T0147053

WHISPERING BODIES

WHISPERING BODIES

A ROY BELKIN DISASTER

JESSE MICHAELS

 SOFT SKULL PRESS

Library of Congress Cataloging-in-Publication Data

Michaels, Jesse, 1969-
Whispering bodies : a Roy Belkin disaster / Jesse Michaels.
pages cm
1. Middle-aged men—Fiction. 2. Neurotics—Fiction.
3. Murder—Investigation—Fiction. 4. San Francisco (Calif.)—Fiction.
I. Title. II. Title: Roy Belkin disaster.

PS3613.I34436W55 2013
813'.6--dc23

2013014413ISBN

ISBN: 978-1-59376-530-9

Cover design by Jesse Michaels
Interior design by Sabrina Plomitallo-González, Neuwirth & Associates

Soft Skull Press
New York, NY

www.softskull.com

Printed in the United States of America

For Audrey

WHISPERING BODIES

There was a website called Helping Hands. The format was questions and answers about spirituality. You could go on there and post a question and other people would post answers.

Deacon asks: Is there more than one Archangel in the bible?
Details: I was just wondering because I saw that there were a lot of angels with names but I wanted to know which ones were archangels.

Under the question there was a column where everybody would post their answers.

PeteK answers: Gabriel.

Sara answers: There is only one archangel: Michael.

Jesusismyanchor answers: Michael and Gabriel.

Most of the questions and answers were from Christians, but some other faiths were also occasionally represented.

Belkin looked at the questions for a long time. He couldn't find the right one to answer. The questions piled up meaninglessly.

Hedgehog asks: Why did the Romans hate Christianity?

MyGodisAwesome asks: Do you realize that you don't deserve the blessings you have?

Jpierce asks: Acts 11:9- "What God hath cleansed, that call not thou common." Any thoughts?

Jenny asks: Is it alright to pray to win a basketball game?

It would be his intuition that would tell him which one to answer. An inner knowing. It took a while. Finally, he saw it:

Splendor asks: Why do they call the taking of the communion "Mass?"

Details: I am a faithful Catholic and I strive to uphold the Apostolic Creed to the best of my mortal ability. Just curious about the meaning of the word "mass."

He thought for a couple of seconds, then started typing.

Belkin124 answers: They call it the Mass because after Jesus was crucified, a mass of people rushed forward to the cross and ate him. Now they eat the wafer to remember it.

He leaned back in his chair, satisfied. Now he could allow himself to *ask* a question. This took a bit more thought. He sat for a while until it came to him and then he typed it all out in one burst.

Belkin124 asks: If God is real, why is there shitting?
Details: It is hateful, violent act! Why does this happen every four days? I resent! Don't say its natural. I WANT TO KNOW WHY COULD GOD MAKE THIS. I mean every weekend church and then pray every night, okay fine. God and Bible and candle. Good. But then in the bathroom- A HORROR! IT COMES OUT LIKE THAT! I AM NOT PROUD OF THAT! WHO COULD LOOK AT IT? I HATE! So then you tell me God? What? How could God do that? That shame?
Also: my wife always lies and plays game with everybody. Her sister is also bich and they are both stealing from me (phone bill and gas card). So how God? What?

The spelling and grammatical errors were intentional. He waited a few minutes for the responses to show up.

Mary answers: Maybe you should worry less about your body and more about your soul. And as for your wife and her sister I don't think that if you are calling her a "bich" that you have very much respect for her.

Samson answers: I have wondered about things like that. Try praying.

Lightofreason answers: You again?

JerryF answers: Do not answer this person's questions. He is a TROLL.

After a few minutes people complained. Still, it took time for the moderators to spot and delete his work. When they deleted his account he would just create a new, higher-numbered *Belkin*. Belkin123, 124, 125. Belkin had been doing this for years.

Jeffrey asks: Who were the Corinthians?

Belkin125 answers: The Corinthians were goat-herding pedophiles who lived on the Greek island known as Maui. Every one of them was an asshole. When Paul came they listened to him because he was the only man they had ever seen who could cook soup. The reason he is always scolding them in his letters is because whenever the Corinthians gathered in groups of more than four people somebody would end up being crucified. This was both the reason for Paul's interest in them and for his eventual abandonment of them.

Violation notice: Belkin125
The Helping Hands community has flagged one of your posts for

violations of the group guidelines. Your account has been suspended. If you feel that this is an error please contact us below.

Roy Belkin called the activity "the Service." It was the central activity of his life. He performed the Service for around two hours each day. By the time he was done he was disoriented and his eyes felt weak. He felt as though the skin on his face had aged. It did not feel good.

There were other things he had to do. Things weren't good in the apartment exactly. At the moment there was too much junk around. He called the accumulation of clutter "the Slow Evil." This was a normal state of affairs. He just couldn't get himself to clean stuff up, generally. In fact, any task at all was difficult. The Slow Evil was a force that never stopped. It was the general deterioration of order.

He was forty-seven years old. Bald, skinny, and pockmarked, he was a man who was likely to be overlooked in most situations. A janitor or a DMV clerk. He had dark, sunken eyes. They did not give him intensity; they gave him a look of anxiety and sleeplessness.

He set up a coffee cup on the shelf by the window. From his bed it was ten feet away. He made some balls out of wet toilet paper and began throwing them at the cup from a seated position on his bed. This wasn't the first time he had made these wet toilet paper balls and he had a name for them: "Thuds." After he had thrown all ten of the Thuds he had made, he collected them from the floor and the cup. He had successfully landed two out of the ten in the coffee cup.

If I can get sixty hits, I will have the power to do the cleaning. Sixty hits. Sixty for power. This was his thinking as he shot the next set of ten. This time he landed three in the cup. After each set he would mark the number of successful shots on a legal pad.

2

3

0

1

4

2 . . .

The process took thirty-five minutes. When it was done, the numbers on the legal pad added up to sixty-two. After he disposed of the Thuds, he rested on his bed and felt the power surging through him. He quickly set to work on the cleaning so as not to waste any of the stored energy. He was successful at cleaning the studio apartment and also doing the dishes that were piled up in the small kitchen alcove.

His apartment was only one large room with an adjoining kitchen and bathroom. Still, it took effort to maintain it. Every day there was another act of maintenance to be performed. Bills, hardware demands, a spilled liquid, cleaning of the bathroom, computer problems, and so on. Usually if Belkin performed one power-building exercise, such as throwing the Thuds into the coffee cup, he could take care of three to five items on his list of tasks.

On this particular day it was time to go shopping. In the top drawer of his dresser was a garment he had made to wear under his shirt. It consisted of a white cloth square with a string affixed to the top corners so that it could be worn around his neck like a one-sided placard. The cloth square was about six by six inches. This inner vestment, called the Shield, was his line of protection against all the horrors of the sidewalk and streets. On the cloth was written a list. Each item was written meticulously, in all capitals, in permanent ink. The list consisted of all the past threats to his safety or mental equilibrium that he had encountered on his trips out of his apartment.

THREATS:
1. APARTMENT FILTH
2. SINGING LADY
3. SKATEBOARD TEENAGER
4. AFRICAN AMERICAN TEENAGER—SHOUTING
5. NEEDY CAT
6. DISGUSTING BIRD
7. DANGEROUS DRIVER—RED TRUCK
8. HOMELESS—MUMBLING
9. HOMELESS—TOUCHING, WANTING
10. TALKING CASHIER
11. HEAT SWEAT
12. "UNMENTIONABLE" PROBLEM
13. LOUD PHONE MAN
14. CRYING PHONE WOMAN
15. FAT STARING MAN WITH GLASSES
14. HOVERING, SCREECHING BIRD
15. AGGRESSIVE INSECT OUTSIDE APARTMENT ENTRANCE
16. CHILDREN ON NEXT DOOR STOOP—WHISPERING

If he was able to include a threat in the list, he would be protected from it—*as long as he was wearing the Shield*. He would feel the cloth on his skin and have that much safety. He called the general problem of the horrors of the outside world "the Pounding." By scanning the inner world of his feelings, he could tell how bad the Pounding was on a given day. He closed his eyes and went within intuitively. *It's a level 8 out there*, he concluded. Even though he had just put it on, he glanced under his shirt at the hanging piece of cloth to make sure it was there.

The Shield was a fairly recent development. He had created it a couple of months ago out of desperation. At that time he had reached a point where he simply could not leave the apartment and he had run out of food. The revolting nature of the outside world was simply too much for him. Finally he had created the Shield as a talisman that guarded against the matter, noise, and unwanted personal interaction that pressed in on his psyche from the raw streets. Though the Shield was a new device, Belkin thought it was one of the greatest things he had ever created. He never appeared outside of his building without it.

There was a faint smell of smoke in the building as he took the elevator down to the lobby, but he was too concerned about the task ahead of him to pay much attention to it. Once outside the building he experienced the usual initial shock. People were everywhere, teeming. A shabby man walked by mumbling to himself. The man's hair was matted and expressed deep resignation. Belkin considered listing the man on the Shield when he got home but it wasn't a direct encounter. Cars tore around corners, women carried red, bleating infants, men in suits shouted into cellular telephones, the electronic bus rambled down its tracks with terrible quietness and speed, seagulls visiting from the beach circled overhead carrying out their unclean missions, puddles of water formed in gutters, melting gum sought his shoes, and the walls of the city were covered with posters, each with an illustration or photograph more terrible than the last one, as if advertising general menace.

The shopping trip came off easily. He was right about the Pounding being a level 8; the city was horrible that day, but none of it touched him on the way to the grocery store or while he was getting his things. If he believed in a God, he would have thanked it for the protective power of the Shield. He was still grateful but he knew that the forces of the universe, both the good ones and the bad, were totally impersonal.

2.

Belkin got back to his apartment building forty-five minutes later. Something terrible had happened. Fire trucks were outside. Black smoke was coming out of a window up on the seventh floor. Police were all over the place. There was yellow tape and harsh ushering going on. He didn't get too near the tape or the pushy men. There were three children he had seen in the past on the stoop next door to his building and he ended up standing near them. He touched the vestment beneath his shirt to remind himself that there was very little the children could do to him. He had seen them *whispering* before on another outing and he had *pre*listed them on the Shield. *Prelisting* meant putting down an incident that had not happened yet. He had envisioned the children whispering about him derisively and marked it on the Shield as a preventative measure.

The children's parents were just inside the door of their building, doing something with hand tools. The mother and father must have been landlords or apartment managers. As for the children, they were *really barely even human yet, in the single digits*, he observed. There were two boys and one girl. They were sitting on the stoop watching the fire- and policemen.

"Hi," one of the boys said to Belkin.

"Hi," said the girl next to the boy, also addressing Belkin.

Belkin nearly dropped the bag of groceries. He turned to answer, knowing that if he ignored them, it was bound to encourage more curiosity, more interaction. "What's going on here?" Belkin asked. He didn't want to know the answer but he thought if he initiated the talk he would catch the children off guard and prevent them from getting the upper hand.

"Something happened," said the girl.

"Do you know what happened?"

The girl just stared at Belkin. Then she leaned over and started whispering in the ear of one of the boys. All three children began laughing.

"Hey! No whispering!" Belkin said. "That's on my list! I've prelisted that!"

The children's father looked out from inside the hall. Belkin tried to smile at him.

A passerby stopped next to Belkin as if he had flagged her

down. He pointedly looked away from her. The woman was flustered and red around the ears. She wore pricey glasses and had a fashionably weeping hairdo. She whined.

"Well, there was a fire," she said to Belkin.

"I would rather not hear any more about it," he responded.

"There's a burned man," she went on.

Belkin ground his teeth.

"The fire was contained. But they say there is somebody dead up there, and detectives are sifting through ashes looking for devices. They think it might be torch-crime."

Belkin quickly got away from her. People who wanted to talk were often drawn to him, though he didn't want to hear about anything. Their words sought his vacuum. Now he was standing closer to his building, looking for a way past the gauntlet of people watching the numerous police officers and firemen. As he stood there, a man walked up to him. Belkin wanted to scream. Why was everybody bothering him?

"Do you live in this building?"

The man had jowly dog flesh. He weighed 230 pounds. His eyes sunk into his face like big bluish marbles dropped into a pudding. His lower lip protruded soggily, a defeated second nose.

"No."

"That's not what I heard," the man said.

"What do you want?"

"I'm Detective Bud Morpello. I'd like to ask you a question."

"What is it?"

"Come to the Mobile Crime Unit over here."

Belkin followed him. The detective walked very slowly. They got into what looked like a converted recreational vehicle that was filled with computers and bulletin boards. The detective sat down in a folding chair that had another chair across from it. Belkin set his groceries down on the floor next to him and sat down. An assistant to the detective wrote his name and contact information on a clipboard and scurried off to one of the computers.

"Do you know what happened?" Detective Bud Morpello asked Belkin.

"No."

"There was a fire."

Belkin said nothing. The two of them stared at each other for a long time. The Mobile Crime Unit was crowded and people fought their way around Belkin and the detective, elbowing each other and shouting. It was becoming clear to Belkin that the man he was talking to was a moron.

"What do you want?" Belkin repeated.

"The fire was arson. There have been three other arsons in the neighborhood. It was the same arsonist," Morpello said. His face registered no emotion, conveyed no significance.

"And? And?!" Belkin said, raising his voice in exasperation.

"A man was killed. A man in an apartment. His name was Frank Relpher. Did you know him?"

"No!"

"He was the maintenance man in the building. He was killed."

"I didn't know him. I have seen a man walking around in over-alls with a tool belt on from time to time."

"So you knew him?"

"No."

"How did you know he was killed?"

"What?"

"You said he was killed. How did you know?" Morpello asked.

"I didn't say that."

Detective Morpello stared at Belkin. His face was rubbery. Belkin felt if he reached out and pinched Morpello's cheek, he could simply pull and stretch the flesh of it six or seven inches from the man's skull and Morpello would just sit there and continue staring.

"Did you know him?" Morpello asked.

"No."

"This isn't going anywhere, Mr. Belking."

"Is that my fault?"

"I'll ask the questions here."

"Go ahead."

"All right, Belking. Let's start with this one. Where were you an hour ago?"

"I was leaving my apartment to go shopping."

Morpello stared listlessly. "Where were you two hours ago?"

"I was in my apartment."

"Where were you three hours ago?"

"I was in my apartment! What is it that you want?"

"Where were you four hours ago?"

"Goddamn it!"

At that moment a harried-looking man tapped on Morpello's shoulder and spoke close to his ear. "Sir, we have the person of significance."

The harried man made a gesture with his chin toward the door of the Mobile Crime Unit. In the doorway was a slender woman wearing a long white dress. She had stringy blonde hair and large wet eyes that were somewhat doleful and sullen. When Belkin looked at her he forgot Morpello, forgot the fire, forgot everything except for her lightness. She seemed to float in the muddle around her like a paper lantern adrift in a swamp.

"All right, Mr. Belking. I've got to ask somebody else a question. I'll talk to you later. Don't take any vacations," Morpello said. "And take this. Call me if you remember anything."

Belkin looked at Morpello for a moment as the man sat there holding his card out. It may as well have been an ape grunting and shaking a tree branch at him. He took the card. Then, as he was led out of the bus, he snuck an aching glance at the vision being led to where he had just been sitting. She caught his eye for a moment. He quickly looked down and noticed that she was clutching a large black book. Embossed on the cover in gold letters were the words MY COMFORT.

Belkin had seen women on the streets with their trinkets, fabrics, babble, tears, vanity, suspicious trips to the bathroom, and shallowly buried animalism. As a race he counted them only slightly less repulsive than men but with the added threat of reproduction. *But this one . . . was . . . different,* he thought as he wandered back toward the building. She looked like wet newspaper, like something made soft by the elements, soon to be dissolved altogether given a few more drops of rain.

He walked back toward the apartment building and waited near the front door. The police and firemen were making final arrangements before letting people return to the building. Belkin overheard people saying that the fire had not spread beyond the apartment in which it had taken place. As he stood there the woman he had seen earlier emerged from the bus. Belkin turned away from her but he could feel her floating toward the doorway of the building. In a moment or two she was by his side, waiting right there with him.

"I saw you in that bus—were they questioning you, too?" she asked Belkin.

"No!" he responded nervously.

There was a brief pause. She had the hungry, shell-shocked look of a dust bowl refugee.

"Why were you in there?"

"I'm a detective!" Belkin shouted.

"Oh . . . " the woman responded.

"Why were you in there?" Belkin asked.

"They found a picture of me in the dead man's apartment," she said. "They said that that makes me a person of significance."

"Ha! As if I didn't know that!"

The police were now letting people in the apartment one by one.

"Well, I imagine I'll be talking to *you* soon," Belkin said. He turned and walked away from her. *Motherfucking asshole motherfucker!* he thought to himself. His detective act had been an uncontrollable fear reaction, but still, it was unforgivable. He checked his mailbox and then took the stairs up to his apartment. He didn't usually take the stairs, but the thought of a balmy, crowded elevator crush after all that he had just been through made him sick to his stomach. In his apartment he tore off his shirt and looked at the Shield. He took it off and put it on his table, a small wooden thing near the window in his studio. It was where he did his thinking. Without wasting any time he got out the pen he used for the Shield. The pen was a fine-point permanent marker. He carefully added three items:

17. CHILDREN—ASKING, LAUGHING
18. ARSON CRIME
19. IDIOT DETECTIVE

After that was taken care of he opened a journal he kept in his desk. He called this book "the Thunder Journal." The entries were sporadic and each was no longer than a sentence or two. This was the book of disasters and miracles only.

JAN. 14-
-THE DAY OF THE FIRE AND THE RELENTLESS POUNDING.
-ENCOUNTERED "SHE."

He thought briefly about hitting the bathtub. That was where he dealt with serious problems and performed level-10 rituals. However, it seemed that the worst was over. He closed the Thunder Journal and climbed into bed. He pulled the covers high against his face and willed himself into a dense black submersion.

Belkin160 asks: Why did Christ hate the children?

Details: My life coach said that Jesus was good except he gave beating to child. Why he did this? He said also that Jesus never had a smile, mostly serious and study the bible and beat the child. He said that Jesus also burned his hand in the desert which angered him and so he punished disciples with laughing and mocking them when they tried to pray. Why he did those things? Also he made the ship sink? Why?

JohnAbbot answers: Hey "Belkin!" We see you here every day! Nobody is fooled by your tricks and jokes! Here's a funny joke: you are going to be facing Him sooner than you think and nobody is going to be laughing. How about trying prayer instead of blasphemy?

IntheGarden answers: Ummm...I don't think so dude. I don't know what book your "life coach" is reading but it's not the bible.

ClaudiaF answers: "With their tongues they have used deceit, the poison of asps is upon their lips." 2Romans

It was his first question of the day. The primary calling of the Service was to ask questions. Once this was taken care of, he could allow himself to answer a question. He decided to answer one. Usually answering one of the questions involved scanning them for a while to find the one that spoke to his soul. On this day he found one that called out to him immediately.

Mountainandfield asks: This Sunday I was baptized for the first time (I have been a Christian for over a year) and I was overcome by a feeling of sadness. What does this mean?

There was already one answer posted:

NathanF answers: Many people have unconventional reactions to baptism. You are crossing a threshold and leaving your old life behind. There is some sadness even though the change is for the better. The joy and blessings you shall receive will more than make up for it.

Belkin thought for three minutes. This was a delicate matter and had to be handled perfectly. Finally he responded.

Belkin126 answers: Did the man try to touch you in any way when you dipped? Like near the groin or on the shining part of your back (low) (the ass)? This happened to me before and I had a lot of feeling about. Don't tell anybody if this happened.

Now he could ask one.

Belkin126 asks: I'm thinking of crucifying somebody (a friend). Advice? Details: I made a cross out of old railroad ties. My friend is agreeable (he is Christian). We want to do it on or around Christmas. Does anybody know where to get really big nails? Also, how do you make a scourge?

He waited for answers.

Guidingstar answers: Why don't you do it in jail because that's where you are going to end up.

Liz answers: "...the wicked shall be cut off from the earth, and the transgressors shall be rooted out of it." Proverbs 2:22

Jarofclay answers: "...they glorified him not as God, neither were thankful; but became vain in their imaginations, and their foolish heart was darkened." - Romans 1:21. Hey buddy, try some Bible for these crazy thoughts you're having: Ps 19:7, Ex. 14:13, Jer. 5:23, Eph 6:11-18, Matt 22:37-39, and especially John 14:6!

His work was interrupted by a knock at the door. He tensed in reaction to the sound. He had never been interrupted while performing the Service before. He shut the computer off and looked through the tiny peephole. The melancholy blonde that he met yesterday was there. He was astonished by both his good and bad luck.

"What do you want?" he shouted. He could feel himself reverting to the ridiculous façade he had created the day before. Part of him was trying to stop, but it was like trying to hold together a vase that was breaking.

"I'm sorry to bother you," she replied.

Belkin opened the door and squeezed through it without letting her see into the apartment. Again, she was wispy and glowing. She backed up as he edged into the hallway. He held the door slightly open behind him.

"You said you're a detective," she said.

"Yes."

"My name is Pernice Balfour."

"Roy Belkin."

There was no handshake. The hall was dark and had a tired carpet with burn marks and other scars. Pernice stood in the poor light clutching the same book she had been carrying the day before and looked up at Belkin plaintively.

"They think I'm a person of significance."

"How did you know which apartment I lived in?" Belkin asked.

"I looked at your box number when you got your mail yesterday after the fire. I thought you might be able to help me—"

"Forget it!" he snapped. "That would be a conflict of interest!"

"You see, they found some things of mine in the burned man's apartment. Which would be fine, except . . . "

"Except what?"

A moth flew around down the hall where the light was pushing its way through a painted-shut window. There was a wrapper from a candy bar under the woman's foot.

" . . . except that I told them I had never met him. I lied about knowing him."

"Why? Why would you lie to us?" Belkin said.

Her eyes were dilated and glistening. "I am a woman of faith," she answered.

"That doesn't explain it! Far from it! That makes it worse!"

"It's just that . . . Frank Relpher and I . . . that was his name, Frank Relpher . . . "

"Yes? Get on with it!"

"We had a brief engagement."

"What is that supposed to mean? An engagement?"

She moaned.

"Snap out of it. Explain yourself!"

"Well, it was before I had become fully committed to my faith, about eight months ago. I met him when he came by my apartment to fix my garbage disposal. We went out a few times. Well, apparently he stole some photographs of me from my house when we were seeing each other. When they asked me about him, I said I didn't know him. It's only because I was trying to forget the whole thing. I didn't know he had the photographs of me in his house or that the police had found them. I know I should not have lied."

"So the police found photographs of you in the burned man's apartment and then you said you didn't know him."

"Yes! You got it exactly right!"

"Well, you've got yourself into quite a situation here!"

"Can you help me?"

"Probably not."

Pernice Balfour looked to be on the verge of tears. Belkin felt a sudden rush of heat around his neck.

"For God's sake! I'll see what I can do. But no more lying!" he said.

"Oh yes! Of course! Thank you, Detective."

"As you know, *illegally*, from reading my mailbox, my name is Roy Belkin. You can call me Belkin."

"Mmm! Yes, Mr. Belkin! Thank you."

"Don't thank me yet. You're still a person of significance."

"Let's to Bible," she said.

"What?"

"Let's to Bible," she repeated and withdrew the large black volume she had been carrying the day before when Belkin saw her in the Mobile Crime Unit. He could tell it was the same book by the title on its cover: MY COMFORT. She clenched her eyes shut and flipped through the pages of the book with her fingers. Finally she stopped shuffling and began reading where she had randomly landed:

"And Lebaoth, and Shilhim, and Ain, and Rimmon: all the cities are twenty and nine, with their villages: And in the valley, Eshtaol, and Zoreah, and Ashnah, and Zanoah, and En-gannim, Tappuah, and Enam, Jarmuth, and Adullam, Socoh, and Azekah, and Sharaim, and Adithaim, and Gederah, and Gederothaim . . . mmm," she concluded.

Belkin was completely lulled by the woman's voice. They both stood there for a moment.

"Lord has words," she said.

"Well, I'll poke around a little bit. I'll contact you if I find out anything further. Until then, don't take any vacations."

He lunged back into his apartment and slammed the door behind him. He wanted to throw himself out the window in penance for the stupid game he had been playing. A fear reaction. *Goddamn me*, he thought.

Soon he was lying in bed remembering her. Her presence was still around, especially in the mental echoes of the things she had said. The Bible recitation had really done something to him. She was very religious but it was a different kind than practiced by those idiots he savaged on the computer every day. She seemed to be without artifice of any kind. Was that possible? Belkin had never even thought about the chance that there could be a human being that wasn't essentially a lying coward. He certainly was. He lost his sense of passing time. The ceiling had cracks in it and was greasy. Why did it look oily? What was that? The overhead light had dead bugs in it. Yet another problem.

As he lay there, Pernice Balfour's lilting voice stayed with him for hours. Every ten minutes or so he would remember his impulsive detective act. "Goddamn it! Goddamn me! Asshole motherfucker!" Then the guilt would be swallowed up by the thought of her again and he would lapse into something that resembled peace.

He resolved to look into it somehow. After all, it was impossible that this woman could have done anything wrong. Of course he would have to disabuse her of the idea that he was involved with the official investigation, but maybe he could do so gently.

4.

It was the next day. Roy decided to go see his father. It was another of the tasks of life, like shopping, that forced one to leave the house, which one just had to do. He hadn't done it in three weeks. He got up and sat at the small table in his apartment. He poured coffee out of the old metal coffeemaker. Roy made coffee at random times, let it sit for a few hours, and then drank it cold at the little table by the window. He could see people wandering by outside if he looked down, or the roof of the building across the street with all its large metal vents and boxes. He wondered what all those ducts and boxes were for as he drank the coffee.

He often marveled at the mechanics of civilization. Who had come up with all these things? The rubber? The plastic? The machines? The computers? All of it? No one person understood all aspects of any single thing such as a building or a computer or a car or what have you. Each complex technical thing had to be a group effort. The real question was *why*? What was the overall design behind all the tinkering? The only answer Roy could come up with was that the basic purpose of humanity, the grand goal of all the individual striving, was to destroy the natural world.

Viewed from an airplane, the human species was certainly, *obviously*, a disease on the planet. Looking down from up there you would see large areas of natural color on the earth and then black patches where there were cities. The black patches were abscesses. From those dark grid clusters thousands of black highway lines would stretch out connecting one to another. At night it would all light up like hot bacteria. Within each dark patch the minds of the human organism generated greater and greater methods of attack against the remaining healthy tissue of the world. This seemed self-evident to Belkin, not a matter of philosophy.

If the purpose of humanity was to destroy the rest of nature, it seemed to be a worthy cause at least. One glance at one of those animal television shows indicated that most of the natural world needed to be put out of its misery. Belkin used to watch one called *Animal Spy* but he became too discouraged after seeing a couple of episodes on the miserable life of the coyote. In general it seemed that animal life was a drama of endless predatory violence, starvation, and encroachment from the human disease grid.

He put on the Shield and his jacket and left the house. There was no power-building ritual needed for the paternal visits. He could just walk out the door and go see the man, probably because of guilt.

He got on the bus and sat next to a window. It was an overcast day. He saw a fat woman with a Doberman. He noticed how boring a mailbox looked. Youths had written graffiti on it. It made the mailbox more boring. He looked closer at the graffiti. BLAST, it said. Why? Next to that was another insignia, this one totally unreadable. What were these kids, three-year-olds? Was there a culture attached to that? These inscriptions looked like urban mind-vomit. What was wrong with the youth? Were they stupid? It was all insane. To take his mind off it he looked at the back of the bus seat in front of him. But there was more graffiti. FUCK YOU, it said. At least that one was a classic.

He got to the stop and then walked a block to his father's apartment. The building was an old, peach-colored, sixteen-unit structure built in the 1950s in the Inner Richmond neighborhood of the city. A nice place to live but not fancy. The rest of the tenants were professionals. He hit the buzzer.

"Yes?"

It wasn't his father. It was one of the agents that looked after his father.

"It's Roy."

The door buzzed open. He walked up the steps. When he got to his father's door the agent opened it before he could knock. It was Agent Hoose. Hoose wore a white shirt and tie with pants.

His hair, blonde, was plastered to his head as if with beeswax. A real hard-on. Still, he never really prevented Roy's visits or bored him with too much bureaucracy. Hoose stood in the door impassively. He was wearing dark glasses.

"What's the nature of this visit?"

"It has no nature."

"That is not sufficient."

"You got that right," Roy responded.

"Let me just ask you: is this a matter of importance? Your father is very absorbed in a project right now, and we want to keep his emotions on the beam."

"Nothing important."

"Let's keep it on the beam."

"The balance beam?"

"The level. The leveling beam."

"You know you guys give me some kind of resistance every time I come here. So why let me visit him at all?" Roy asked the question partially out of a secret hope that one of these days he would be disallowed from visiting his father.

"We think that the presence of family has a stabilizing influence. We classify you as a Necessary Deficient."

"Oh."

"Are you still receiving your checks?"

"Yes," Roy answered.

Hoose didn't follow the question with anything.

Roy walked past him down the hall. A short woman in a dress with a rag in her hand noticed him.

"Roy! Little Roy!" She came into the hall and embraced him warmly. She was a heavyset woman in her late sixties.

"Hello, Ms. Calbenza."

"God gives me big gift when you came in! The gift are *you*! You a bless!"

"Thank you, Ms. Calbenza."

"Oh bless the heaven!"

"Where is my father?"

"You am a good boy! Good Christ give the bless!"

"Thank you, Ms. Calbenza."

"Mr. Belkin are in the living room."

Roy walked into the living room, glad to shake Calbenza. As a young child, Roy had been raised by her. As an adult, he didn't want to get involved.

Ulmers Belkin was in the living room. He was seventy-four years old. He had sandy hair that resisted graying. Instead it remained wooden blonde, although his face had given in to the years like a dried egg. He wore a Hawaiian shirt and had the look of a veteran beach bum. Somebody who used to do things in tents in the seventies. A rotten Beach Boy. Somebody who used to belong to a cult or maybe even run one. Actually he was none of those things, but that's what he looked like.

He had several computers on the coffee table in front of him. The computers were wired to other, smaller devices—black and silver boxes, exposed grid circuits, small transmitters. Belkin wondered how his father set these systems up. He knew from experience only that he did it on the fly, always reconfiguring the gear. His father's mind was inside the boxes.

"Hello, Roy. You know I can't talk about the project I'm working on—it's a bit confidential, to tell you the truth."

His father had said some variation of the same thing to him

every time he had seen Roy for the last thirty or forty years. If Roy spoke back or initiated any conversation, there would be no response. Roy sat there watching him for about five minutes and then spoke up.

"So how are you, Dad?"

It was a matter of ritual. Ulmers looked at the wall for a moment and then went back to work. Roy noticed that he looked at the wall every two minutes or so. Even that gesture was not a response to Roy speaking but rather just something Ulmers did with his head from time to time.

Roy stayed there for twenty minutes. His father spoke to himself and fiddled around with the computer. Then Roy got up. He nodded to Agent Hoose on the way out. Hoose was in the kitchen doing something with his hands in a briefcase. Hoose looked up and nodded.

"How's it going, Hoose?"

Hoose didn't respond.

"Or should I say 'Hoose it going?'"

"Not funny, Junior."

"Is my father all right? Is he doing what you want?"

"We provide a stable environment for him, and yes, he continues to support our efforts. That's why we also provide a stipend for you. We consider you an Orbiting Significant for the Principal."

"Always like to remind me that I'm on the payroll, don't you?"

Hoose said nothing.

"Have you cracked the big code?" Roy said.

Hoose stared at him from behind the dark glasses. Roy went on.

"Have you figured out the metacode? The big answer? The very reason that we are all eating each other's shit?"

"Maybe we have, Roy," Hoose answered without smiling.

"Thank God," Roy said.

Roy walked out. He liked Hoose. If he prodded him long enough, Hoose would always consent to exactly one almost-joke. Roy knew better than to push him beyond that. After the single almost-joke the steel doors crashed shut, and to ask for more was dangerous. The times Roy had pushed Hoose too far, his monthly check had been docked.

On the bus ride home he felt light-headed, as he always did after these visits. He tried not to think about it. He now wished openly that the agents would prevent him from visiting, but he couldn't stop going on his own—the guilt. He would be back in two weeks to try again.

His father, one of the greatest cryptologists on the planet, had been discovered by the government long before Roy was born. Ulmers had been a child prodigy code breaker during the Cold War. As Ulmers Belkin grew older, he kept working for ever more shadowy intelligence organizations. Belkin's mother had been somebody his father worked with in eastern Europe in the fifties. Presumably she was taken in by his brilliance. It seemed likely that Ulmers was still able to communicate at that time. All Roy knew about her was that her name was Nadja and that she had left his father because he lost his mind. Roy didn't know why he had ended up with his father rather than with his mother. He didn't remember her, and the agents had changed since then, so nobody knew anything.

His father was lost in calculation, forever. It was over for him. A neat escape. Technologies had changed over the years but they always seemed to have a use for Ulmers Belkin. The aging savant operated in a field that Roy had heard Agent Hoose refer to as "metacode."

Roy grew up in fifteen different countries, in safe-houses that were little more than encampments. There were always operatives around. The housekeeper, Ms. Calbenza, had appeared sometime in the 1960s, perhaps in the Carribean somewhere, but Roy couldn't remember exactly. She was a domestic who had been brought into the fold to take care of Ulmers and Roy. Everywhere the three of them went—Korea, Guam, Mexico, various countries in Europe, Haiti, Japan—his father worked with electronic equipment and notebooks among packs of mysterious and boring men. Meanwhile, Ms. Calbenza always managed to find a church that she would drag Roy to. The churches she chose were often ones that featured snake handling, foaming, encircling, yelling, hugging, gibberish, and disease rallies. Services would take place as many as three times a week. His father floated around the house in a trance, tethered to electronic equipment and piles of handwritten and typed documents. Roy read in his room or listened to Ms. Calbenza reading the Bible or went with her to one-room churches filled with people who were devout and hysterical.

As far as his monthly stipend went, Roy had been living under this arrangement since he had become an adult. To keep everything stable, the agency or whatever it was that employed his father sent Roy a check each month that covered his living expenses. The check was never late. The amount was currently $2,830.00 and it went up by 2 percent per year. Roy called his father's employers "the Entity." Roy had never had an emergency, but he imagined that if he did, the Entity would cover it.

The bus plodded up the steep angles back to his neighborhood. A memory emerged, one he hadn't thought of for years. It was a recollection of the last time Roy's father had connected with Roy.

He knew that it was in the Philippines. That was a place they had stayed for more than one year, so he remembered it better than some of the other countries they had visited. It was in a small house. He was seven years old or so. He remembered that it was late afternoon. His father walked in. Roy was reading on the floor. His father kneeled down in front of him. Roy was surprised because his father rarely engaged with him. This time was different. Ulmers spoke directly to his son.

"You see, Roy, here's what you do." He was unbuttoning his shirt.

Roy sat there.

Ulmers went on. "What you do, Roy, is you write things down that could cause trouble."

Ulmers now had his shirt open and he was showing Roy a cloth garment hanging from his neck. Even as a young boy, Roy could tell that his father had made the cloth shield himself. Behind the cloth shield Roy saw that his father had a gauze bandage completely encircling his midsection. There was a faint red spot on one side of the bandage. The shield dangled out of his father's shirt over the bandaged area as he held it forward so that Roy could see it.

"If you write it down on this shield, it can't hurt you," Ulmers continued.

In his mind's eye Roy still remembered his father's shield. He could mentally read the item that he had read as a seven-year-old:

8. MAN IN MARKET WITH SANDALS CARRYING KNIFE UNDER NEWSPAPER.

There were several other items preceding this one on the list, but if Roy had read them, he couldn't remember them. His father stared at him intently as if checking to see if Roy comprehended. Roy nodded.

After that day Roy had nightmares about a man with one hand tucked into the folds of a newspaper, always sidestepping toward him through a bustling crowd. The bad dreams had continued through his childhood but eventually dissipated. Roy had created his own shield only recently. Roy had no assassins stalking him, but he found that the world had other ways of rattling a person. He had been pleasantly surprised by how well the Shield worked. *As you get older, you realize how much of what your parents told you as a child was actually true*, he thought. Though in his case, the transmission of the Shield was one of the very few child-parent interactions he had experienced at all.

The bus pulled to a stop and Roy got up.

He walked up the street toward his house. There were slopes. People were getting out of cars and getting into cars. There was an airplane somewhere. People had bags. He could hear the beeping of a truck backing up. The city blasted his nerves as he walked home. He had no illusions about his paranoia. He knew that in spite of the world's ills, his bad feelings came from the inside, not the outside. The fact that the world outside his apartment triggered his fear was because the fear was there to be triggered—it was latent. He also knew that he suffered from narcissistic isolation but he couldn't think of a solution. His dislike of the human game had gone far beyond normal alienation. He couldn't even begin to imagine "reaching out."

He opened the door to his apartment. Inside, the Slow Evil was beginning to gain a foothold. There was a coffee cup, some loose pencils, a pair of pants, a battery package. He sat down at his table and began to devise a power-building ritual to deal with the Slow Evil.

Homicide Connected with Fourth Arson in Western Addition

The San Francisco Police Department has confirmed that the Pierce St. building that was the target of an arson attack on Tuesday was also the scene of a murder that occurred just before the fire took place. In addition, arson investigators have stated that Tuesday's fire in the Western Addition was "almost certainly" set by the same person or persons as three other arson incidents that have occurred around the city in the last six months.

In a grim variation on a scenario San Francisco residents are beginning to become accustomed to, the

Pierce St. apartment building's handyman, Frank Relpher, was shot and killed in his apartment just prior to the arson. Relpher lived in the apartment in which the fire was set. A source close to the investigation has told the Chronicle that police believe the arsonist broke into Relpher's apartment, was surprised by him and fatally shot him just before setting the blaze. The perpetrator set the fire in the area where the victim's body was found, presumably to destroy the evidence.

"The investigation is somewhat complicated by the fact that the murder scene is also a fire scene, so what we are engaged in now is a painstaking forensics process," Investigator Ron Nesbitt stated at Tuesday's press conference. Mayor Newsom promised to "Redouble efforts, divert funding and pull out all the stops" in the investigation of the string of arsons. "We have already had this matter at the top of the list as far as the (police) department goes and the fact that the arsonist

is now suspected of murder makes the situation that much more urgent," he stated. Tuesday's fire resulted in relatively minor damages to the building thanks to the quick action of neighbors but it was the first incident to be connected with a loss of life.

The murder victim, 56-year-old San Francisco native Frank Relpher, lived and worked in the Pierce St. apartment building for over ten years. Members of the public who knew Relpher have been asked to come forward, as the deceased man had no known family or close personal friends. Landlord Rani Hamalarmakh stated that Relpher was a "competent guy" who was adept at whatever repairs were required around the building. "He came with the place when I bought it," Hamalarmakh told the Chronicle. "Nobody really knew him. But he was always good when you needed to unclog a drain or hang a door."

Belkin dropped the newspaper on the floor. Before reading the article he hadn't heard that the man found in the burned apartment upstairs had been shot beforehand. He realized that the whole idea of Pernice Balfour being a "person of significance" was even more absurd than he initially thought. She was no killer, and if she had lied to the police about knowing this Frank Relpher guy, so what? He dismissed the problem from his mind. Surely they would come to the same conclusion.

As usual, Belkin spent the next two hours doing his daily work on his computer. He got some good thoughts in. After he performed the Service he looked around the room. It was two o'clock. The afternoon was always the time of confrontation, of fighting off responsibilities. The Slow Evil seemed to be getting faster. There were new piles and misplaced objects. The great insult of clutter was spreading itself like a lazing animal. As was often the case, he couldn't summon the energy to do anything about it. He sat on his bed staring at the gathering mess. His power was low. He suspected that this had something to do with Pernice Balfour because he had more or less been in a trance since meeting her.

He kept three ice cube trays in the freezer. He removed them, dumped their contents into the toilet, and waited. After ten minutes he thrust his arm into the freezing water and held it under until he couldn't stand it anymore. *This is harder than people realize,* he thought to himself. Next he did it with the other arm and counted slowly to forty. It demanded prodigious endurance. Finally he submerged his feet, both at once, taking them out only when he felt as though he was beginning to show signs of hypothermia. They came out white and buzzing. It was a power-generating exercise called "Going into the Bowl."

After doing it he was able to clean the bathroom and make a trip to the laundry room. By the time he was done with everything it was five o'clock. On nights like this, when he had accomplished most of what he had set out to do, he generally waged more computer attacks or watched one of several movies that he owned. But on this night he simply lay on his bed and became preoccupied with mental images of Pernice Balfour. He rested his hands on his skull. They were cold. He wondered if they were still that way from their journey into the bowl a couple of hours ago. He contemplated his baldness for a few moments with his fingers crossed over the dome of his head. It made no difference to him really. What hair he had was always short, trimmed once every three months by the semicatatonic barber down the street. A veteran of Manzanar internment camp, the barber was eighty years old, Japanese, and half-dead. He was the only human being whom Belkin could stand to have touch him.

The phone rang.

"Detective Belkin?"

"Yes."

"It's Pernice Balfour."

"Yes?"

"I'm calling you from jail!"

"What?"

"They arrested me!"

"What?"

"They found some things in my apartment . . . "

"What kind of things? What's going on?"

"They found some kind of arson stuff and they also found . . . I can hardly believe this . . . they found a gun!"

"What were you doing with that stuff in your apartment?"

"It's not mine! Somebody must have put it in there!"

Belkin couldn't think of anything to say. He felt shock, which registered as nothingness, and also a great sense of happiness that he was back on the case. The latter feeling filled him with remorse and he made a mental note to spend several hours punishing himself for it at some later time.

"Ms. Balfour, don't say anything to the police!"

"But I'm already talking to you!"

"I'm not a normal police officer exactly—actually, I'm a *freelance* detective . . . "

"Well . . . all right. I've already said a lot to them, to tell you the truth. I mean, I answered their questions. But I couldn't tell them anything. What could I tell them? I don't know where that stuff came from. They found it in my closet. I didn't put it in there!"

"I'm going to come down there."

Belkin heard sobbing. He looked at the phone, not knowing why he was doing it. He thought he saw pinkish-gray steam coming out of the receiver. A stress hallucination.

"Mr. Belkin . . . "

"Yes?"

"You can visit in the morning. I'm in jail number 8."

Belkin went to sleep.

The next morning he took a cab to County Jail number 8 on Seventh Street. Typically it took hours for him to force himself out of the house but today it was unusually easy. Maybe having an altruistic motive helped or maybe he was just smitten with the woman, he thought as he put his shirt on over the Shield. Since the last time he had worn it he had remembered an ugly incident from a few years earlier and had added JUGGLING IMBECILE to the list.

Jail number 8 was where they housed the female prisoners. The building had small, bleak windows. The winter sun in San Francisco was dark. He had to go through a metal detector. The man screening him was balding, skinny, and dejected. He wore a bland gray uniform and his eyes were listless. He looked like a person who smoked cigarettes all night. A human weed. Belkin and the man realized that they looked like one another and both glanced away. In a reception area, Belkin had to sign in. The people would file into a visiting room in groups of eight. He had to wait for an hour.

Finally Belkin and Pernice were seated at a card table alongside the other visitors and inmates. Two female guards hovered nearby. The guards seemed to be there especially to watch Pernice, as only one other guard covered the entire rest of the visitation room.

"Thank you for coming, Detective Belkin!"

She was wearing an orange outfit with the letters *SFC* stamped on the back.

"Never mind that. Tell me what happened. Don't leave out any details."

"I can just tell you what they told me . . . they questioned me and told me a few things but they haven't explained everything. The police received an anonymous letter telling them to look in my bedroom closet. I guess they got it the day after Frank was killed. The reason they followed up on it was that the letter had some details that only somebody who knew about the murder could know. That's what they told me, but they wouldn't tell me exactly what the letter said. I couldn't believe it when they showed up at my house. I was just reading my Bible. They asked me if they could come in. I let them in."

"That was your first mistake."

"Well, they went straight to my bedroom closet and went digging around in there. That closet is a bit of a sin area for me. I stuff everything in there. Anyway, they started pulling everything out. I was just sitting there watching them. They dug all the way to the bottom of all the things in there and they found a box with a gun and some chemicals in it. Then they arrested me. When they questioned me, they told me that it was the same type of gun that Frank Relpher was killed with."

"What kind of chemicals did they find?"

"I don't know. But they said that they thought it was the same stuff that was used to start all those fires."

Belkin looked at the portable table they were sitting at. The plastic surface of it was scratched up as if people sat there clawing at it while they talked to one another. He tried to come up with a reasonable tack to pursue, but he was a bit lost. Balfour was swimming in the jail jumpsuit like a blonde otter in a sewage overflow. His mind began wandering. *How such a being could be produced by this cesspool of a world*, Belkin thought, *only God knows. Or would know if there was a God. Actually even if there were a God, He probably wouldn't know, because a God anywhere near this vile planet would have to be either indifferent or just completely amoral. Like one of those Roman gods.*

What was the name of the one that raped peasants and struck goats blind and so on? Zeus? Now there's a God a man can believe in.

Finally he snapped out of it.

"Tell me about your relationship with Frank Relpher."

Pernice clutched at something. Belkin saw that she had come up with another Bible somehow.

"He came by my apartment to fix my garbage disposal about eight months ago. I told you that already, right?"

"It's fine, just go on."

"I was not fully committed to the Lord yet when I met him. He asked me if I would like to go to the movies with him. I saw him four or five times after that. At that time I was just starting to work at Our Father's House. That's a soup kitchen over on Eighteenth Street where I volunteer. Anyway, I got the Huge Blessing about two weeks after I met Frank. I told him I couldn't go on seeing him. Actually, I'm embarrassed to tell you this, but he didn't take it very well. He would stop by all the time or call me, kind of like he thought I would change my mind or something. Finally I told Father Basil, the priest who runs the soup kitchen. Well, he was kind enough to come by the building and talk to Frank. Frank was raised Catholic and I think having a priest tell him not to bother me convinced him because I didn't hear from him after that. And that was all that happened," she said.

"What was Frank Relpher like?"

"Oh, I don't know. He didn't talk much. He was sort of boring, really. I can tell you one thing, he didn't like people. Whenever we would encounter anybody, he would complain about them. I mean the waiter, the guy in traffic, people in the building, he hated everybody. That's one of the reasons I cut it off with him. I couldn't help but wonder when he would start hating me. But really, I just didn't care for him in *that* way, if you know what I mean."

"Hmm. You said you got 'the Huge Blessing' about two weeks after you met Frank. What does that mean? What is the Huge Blessing?"

Pernice's eyes widened and her face changed colors.

"That's when Lord tooketh what wath hith."

"Huh?"

"The Lord tooketh my soul upon hith mantel and verily I wath transformed."

"Oh. Of course," Belkin affirmed. *Why does she suddenly have a lisp?* he wondered. Then he realized that her speech was taking on a heightened religiosity as she spoke of sacred matters.

"Are you a man of faith?"

"Yes, I most certainly am."

"That's wonderful!" Pernice whispered urgently. "Lord is with us! How wonderful that he sent me one of our own! You don't usually see a detective who is also a man of faith!"

Pernice looked ecstatic. Belkin was too happy with his success with her to worry about the ever-deepening hole he was digging himself into.

"No, you are right. I consider my work in the field of detection to be secondary really. I mean, all that I ever really detect is *His Spirit*, when it comes right down to it."

"OOHHH!"

"Listen, Pernice, tell me more about how this Relpher fellow got the photographs of you. You said the police found some photographs of you in Relpher's apartment? And that you had never given him any?"

"Oh, yes. That's another thing. Frank went into my apartment when I wasn't there. Those photographs were taken from an album that I never showed to him. You know, he could go into any of the apartments. He was the manager of the building, or at least he was the maintenance man. So anyway, yes, he went into my apartment and he must have been there long enough to dig around and find them."

At that moment an electronic tone sounded over the intercom.

"That means we only have two more minutes," Pernice said.

"All right, we'll wrap it up. I think my next step will be to talk to the police officer who questioned you."

Pernice wailed. "Would you like to drink of Bible?"

"I thought you would never ask."

She performed the same ritual that she had at the apartment building, flipping the book open with her eyes closed and shuffling through the pages randomly.

"What are you doing?" Belkin asked.

"I let Lord help me find the right passage. The right passage is always the one that *He* wants to hear, not the one that I want to read."

"Finally a woman who talks sense."

"Ah, here," she said rapturously. "Mr. Belkin, I always seem to find the page so quickly when you are around." She opened her eyes and peered down at where she had landed. "And he shall bring the bullock unto the door of the tabernacle of the congregation before the LORD; and shall lay his hand upon the bullock's head, and kill the bullock before the LORD.

And the priest that is anointed shall take of the bullock's blood and bring it to the tabernacle of the congregation: And the priest shall dip his finger in the blood, and sprinkle of the blood seven times before the LORD, before the vail of the sanctuary. And the priest shall put some of the blood upon the horns of the altar of sweet incense before the LORD, which is in the tabernacle of the congregation; and shall pour all the blood of the bullock at the bottom of the altar of the burnt offering, which is at the door of the tabernacle of the congregation . . . mmm."

"Wow," Belkin said.

"Yes, He is," Pernice responded.

With that a voice came over the loudspeaker informing visitors and prisoners that their time was up.

Belkin walked down Seventh Street thinking about it. Somebody had killed Relpher and then broken into Pernice's apartment and buried the materials in her closet. It was a sick, disgusting, vile, nauseating world full of scum-filth and perverts. He was tired of it. Tired, tired. He felt his forehead sinking into his eyelids. He flagged down a cab with both hands. The gesture was awkward and absurd. Not only was the world a swamp but also every movement he made it in was out of place and stilted. He was an offensive alien in a plane of colliding waste-material. Whether that material was the inanimate garbage collecting on the outskirts of every city or the biological-human garbage rushing around, building expressways, and committing acts of murder within the city made little difference.

But Pernice seemed different. Of course she was naïve, but her intentions were like water coming out of a rock. Belkin dealt with other religious types every day when he performed the Service, but they were all frauds compared to her. Their fear and desire for belonging was pathetically transparent. Pernice struck him as genuine. Naturally, somebody had honed in on her innocence and attacked. She had been framed. There was no other possibility. Riding in the cab through the Financial District, watching the people dashing around, he resolved to remove the blemish that had been projected onto her even if he had to take the blame for it *himself*. As he was having these thoughts, he witnessed a moment of intimacy between a man and a woman in business clothing. They were exchanging a kiss as the woman was about to walk into an office building. Her hand made a furtive grab for her boyfriend's crotch when they embraced. "Scum!" Belkin whispered angrily against the window as his cab plodded down Larkin Street.

6.

Later that day, after doing his work on the computer, he decided to work on "the case." He got out some yellow paper and jotted down initial notes:

1. WHO DID IT
2. WHY DID THEY DO IT
3. WHY DID THEY CHOOSE PERNICE FOR THE FRAME UP

4. DID PERNICE KNOW THE KILLER

5. DID RELPHER KNOW THE KILLER

6. WHY IS THIS WORLD SUCH A GOD-FORSAKEN SHITHOLE

7. WILL HE STRIKE AGAIN

8. CAN I SOLVE THIS OR APPEAR TO SOLVE IT

Belkin didn't know the answer to any of the questions. It seemed logical to try to appeal to the homicide investigators and simultaneously see if he could shake them down for a little information. That strange detective had given him his card in the Mobile Crime Unit. He called the number on the card and got the homicide division. He told the person who answered the phone that Detective Morpello had told him to call if he remembered anything.

"Would you like me to take a message telling Detective Morpello what you remembered?"

"No, I want to talk to him."

"Hold on."

A recording of public transit safety advice came on. Then somebody answered.

"Hello?" The voice was slow and sounded like a person with an enlarged tongue.

"Hello, Detective Morpello?"

"Hello?"

"Hello? Detective Morpello? This is Roy Belkin . . . "

"Huh?"

"This is Roy Belkin! The man you interviewed on Pierce Street . . . "

"Who?"

"I'm trying to tell you! I am the man that you spoke to . . . "

"Huh?"

"Goddamn it! I'm the man you spoke to on the day of the fire!"

"Who?"

"I'm the man that you interviewed in the Mobile Crime Unit! The Mobile Crime Unit! DO YOU REMEMBER THE MOBILE CRIME UNIT?"

"Huh?"

"Listen to me! Listen to me! I-AM-THE-MAN-WHO-YOU-SPOKE-TO-AT-THE-SCENE-OF-THE-ARSON."

"What?"

"NEVER MIND! I'LL COME DOWN THERE IN PERSON!"

"That's good. I'll tell them to send you in when you get here."

Belkin slammed the phone down on the receiver.

Hot with rage, Belkin threw on his coat, barely remembering the Shield, and headed out the door. The cab he took to the police station smelled of menthol, warm plastic, and vomit. He climbed out of the vehicle and almost flung the money at the driver in disgust. He was as angered by being forced to enter the world at large again as by anything else. Belkin had avoided leaving his house more than once a week for five years. Now he had made two extra trips out of his apartment within three days.

Apparently Morpello had authorized the visit because besides handing him a sheet of paper on a clipboard filled with tedious questions, there was little bureaucratic opposition to him seeing the detective. They did manage to make him wait forty-five minutes, however. As he sat there he realized he didn't really have much of a pretext for seeing Morpello. Eventually a desk clerk led him to the detective's office.

"Morpello! Do you recognize me now?"

"Huh?"

Bud Morpello looked up from a pile of papers on his desk. The room smelled like coffee grounds and old upholstery. What light came through the drawn blinds was halfhearted. The detective's features seemed to have given in to gravity even more than the first time Belkin had seen him. Heavyset and pockmarked, Morpello sat behind his desk staring at a pile of papers listlessly.

"Detective Morpello! I'm here to talk to you about the murder of Frank Relpher!"

"I know you—you lived in his building."

"Yes!" Belkin shouted.

"Did you know him?"

"Listen: I am a friend of Pernice Balfour's."

"Who?"

"I wanted to ask you a couple of questions about the woman you have in custody."

"I'll ask the questions here," Morpello said.

"Fine."

There was a long pause. The pause was long enough for Belkin to think about other things and then come back to what was going on. They seemed to be staring at each other but Belkin wasn't sure because the room was so dark. For all he knew, Morpello could have been asleep or dead. Belkin couldn't stand it anymore.

"Well are you going to ask any questions or not?"

"Who are you?" Morpello finally asked.

"I'm Roy Belkin. We spoke on the phone about an hour ago."

"That was you?"

"Yes! Why do you think I'm here?"

"I thought that was somebody else."

"Anyway, look. I think you have the wrong person. I know that woman and she's not the kind of person that burns buildings and kills people!"

"Oh," Morpello said.

"Also, I found out something about this Frank Relpher. He sometimes went into people's apartments without asking. I mean, that's how he had the photographs of Pernice Balfour. That's why she is the person of significance, right? Because he had photos of her in his apartment? But did it ever occur to you that he could have stolen them? I'm just saying, there's more to this than meets the eye. Somebody else may have had a reason to kill him. I think somebody set up Pernice Balfour."

"Are you talking about the Bible lady?"

"Yes."

"Oh."

"What did you find in her apartment exactly?" Belkin asked.

"I can't answer that."

"You can't or you won't?"

"I don't know."

Silence returned to the room. He could hear people bustling around outside the small office but there was no activity in Morpello's little quadrant. The lack of sound or any other stimulus went on and on. Finally, Belkin just got up and left. Morpello sat behind his desk in the dark without reacting. How the man had become a detective was beyond comprehension.

Belkin walked out into the series of cubicles and phone banks that comprised the police station. It was much calmer than he had imagined it would be. He was so conditioned by years of television that he had assumed there would be people bustling around handing mug shots to one another and arrestees jawing with prostitutes and beat cops. Instead it looked more or less like a post office. As he was leaving, a man sidled up next to him and took his arm.

"Hey—I remember you from the building fire."

The man was short, slender, and dark. He was much less bald than Belkin. His nose looked like a natural rock formation that might be found on a mountain range—one of the geological noses of the Old World. This fellow was very much of the city, however. He had black curly hair and a tight lavender shirt. There was something too familiar about the arm grab. Belkin pulled away phobically.

"Yes?"

"You came here to talk to Morpello, huh?"

"Who are you?"

"I'm the crime scene photographer, Emile LeCroix. And you are a fascinating man. May I take your photo?"

"Absolutely not!"

Belkin tried to brush by, but the photographer did a quick side-step and blocked his exit.

"If you want to know more about this case, I can tell you all about it."

"I don't."

"Frank Relpher was not a normal man," LeCroix said. He had several days' growth of beard. The five o'clock shadow was sculpted around the edges, giving it a stylish, manicured look. It disgusted and irritated Belkin.

"Leave me alone!"

"The crime scene yields much bounty in this case," LeCroix went on insinuatingly. He spoke as though he was telling Belkin about a secret brothel, leaning toward him and partially covering his mouth. Belkin actually *did* want information, but this LeCroix rubbed him the wrong way. There was something lurid about him. "Sometimes you have to go right to the wasp's nest to get the honey, if you know what I mean," he continued in an oily whisper.

"I don't know what you mean."

"Oh, so we're playing *that* game," LeCroix said, and winked. "For your sake I just hope that you weren't involved in this in any way, because Bud Morpello always gets his man."

"I certainly wasn't! And as for Detective Morpello, that man is an idiot!" Belkin shouted.

A couple of people turned at the outburst. One man seated nearby got up from his desk.

"Sir, watch your mouth. Detective Bud Morpello is the best goddamned cop in this city."

Belkin forced himself not to respond. There was something wrong with these people—all of them. As he had the thought he noticed that LeCroix was wearing obscenely tight pants that bunched up around his crotch. A camera hung around his neck as low as his navel on a long silver cord. Belkin headed for the door. He sensed LeCroix leering at him from behind.

●●●

Once at home, he added two items to the Shield:

20. REVOLTING TAXI
21. DEGENERATE CRIME SCENE PHOTOGRAPHER

He took off his shirt and lay down on the kitchen floor. It was obvious he was making no progress in "the case." He was utterly spent from going out over and over again. He didn't fear failure so much as losing interest due to lack of headway. An hour later he was still on his back. He lapsed into half sleep. Many of his best ideas came in that state, right there on the kitchen floor. He directed his fuzzy, semiconscious thought toward the problem of the Pernice Balfour frame-up.

Among the power-building rituals that Belkin used to generate motivation, there was a very special one that he reserved for situations that needed maximum psychic energy. This ritual was called "the Prometheus Vow." He had used it only twice in his life, once to get himself to go shopping more often and once to limit masturbation. The Prometheus Vow was a level-10 ritual. He decided that this situation was dire enough to invoke it. The last time he performed it, it had nearly killed him.

He brought some canned food into the bathroom. The process of the Prometheus Vow was simple but demanding: he would light four votive candles, place them at the corners of his bathtub, and remain in the tub until they burned out. The candles lasted for about twenty-four hours each. During this time he would recite a vow thirty times each waking hour. Sleep was permitted, just not departure from the bathtub. He would write the vow beforehand. Belkin didn't know how these rituals came to him but he recognized them as revealed truth. He took a few minutes to articulate the covenant he would be reciting in the tub. He wrote the words in ballpoint pen on a yellow legal pad.

I VOW TO DO ALL IN MY POWER TO UNCOVER THE TRUTH ABOUT PERNICE BALFOUR AND TO RESTORE HER TO THE LEVEL OF PUBLIC DECENCY SHE ENJOYED BEFORE SHE WAS SET UP AND FRAMED BY THE FILTHY LYING MURDERER.

He read the vow a couple times. He decided it was pretty good.

He took an hour to gather his resolve. It was five o'clock when he started. As he had experienced the other two times he underwent the Prometheus Vow, the first few hours in the tub were relatively easy. The water was pleasant. He recited the vow. The daylight hours passed. The trouble began at nine that night with pain in his neck. He drifted off to sleep around midnight, mumbling the last cycle of the vow for the day. He had a pillow between his head and the rim of the tub and his hands were at rest on his chest to avoid early sogging.

At 4:00 AM he woke up freezing. He shot hot water into the tepid pool he had been sleeping in. His neck had gotten worse. He had every towel in the house to bolster his body in various ways, scaffolding it away from the tub, which became painfully difficult over extended periods. Over and over he said the vow in the dark with the rush of water loud behind it.

At dawn he had a can of cocktail onions and tried to keep his arms elevated while he said the words. Daylight made its way into the bathroom. He got into a rhythm: change the water, say the vow, do stretching exercises, adjust the towel, count to eight hundred, start over. The morning passed slowly. The great agony of asceticism is temptation. *I have done enough, these vows never really work, I am verging on real physical injury, I can go to bed for an hour and come back*—the lies paraded through his consciousness. Then came boredom, depression, and despair. He said the vow mechanically.

"I vow to do all in my power to uncover the truth about Pernice Balfour . . . "

In absorption, his mind traveled to weird areas. Even as he repeated the vow in his mind his imagination wandered inward. He saw decapitations, flayings, infanticides, and prison rapes. Darkness and horror seem to be the bottom line of the subconscious. Then back to the vow. It would feel as if an hour had gone by and then he would look at the clock and see that it had been only ten minutes. The candles kept burning. Finally at around three in the afternoon of the next day, one candle went out. It took another three hours for the others to go. He stood up for the last bit of it, barely hanging on. The floor was covered with trash, bags of food, wet towels, and the expired candles. As the smoke from the last one dissipated he said the vow one more time and limped over to his bed. It had taken twenty-six hours.

A few days later, Belkin was at the corner store, a place called Sapik's. He walked through the tight, dark aisles. The poorly lit shop had an air of dissolution. It was a small convenience store that mainly traded in liquor and cigarettes. Belkin looked at the bags of chips. Among them was a product called "Pork Rinds." He wanted to take them off the shelf and stuff them in a garbage can somewhere. What the hell was that? Why did these corner stores always have that? "Pork Rinds." Disgusting!

He brought his purchase up to the counter. It was scouring powder. Sapik himself was behind the register, as always. Sapik was a short Indian man with a beard. He was listening to a cassette tape and repeating back sounds he heard on it. The sounds seemed inhuman.

"*HunyeeeeeAAARRRRRuuuuhhhhWOOOO,*" the tape said.

"*HunyeeeeeAAARRRRRuuuuhhhhWOOOO,*" Sapik repeated back as he rang up Belkin's purchase.

Belkin looked on. Sapik was one of the few people he liked.

"Studying Cave Urdu?" Belkin asked.

Sapik stared at him. "You must be kidding."

Belkin stood there with his scouring powder now in a paper bag.

"Who told you to ask me that?" Sapik said. "My daughter? She told you? Right? Jenny, right? You are very funny."

"No," Belkin responded.

"There are only three hundred people in the world who speak this language. I find it hard to believe that you happen to be familiar with it."

"Suit yourself," Belkin said, collecting his change. He walked out into the sunlight with one finger on the Shield beneath his shirt. The truth was that his father had been a student of the world's most obscure languages. Ulmers had studied several of them closely in one of his code projects more than thirty years ago. A genius, the man had learned rudimentary Navajo, Inuit, and Icelandic in the space of a few years. Cave Urdu had been one of the languages that had engaged Ulmers the longest, taking up almost three years of his attention. In the end his father's overseers had abandoned the project because they found that even though

Cave Urdu was the ultimate code language, it caused dizzy spells and rage attacks in people who tried to learn it.

He walked along with his single grocery listlessly. He was depressed. After finishing the Prometheus Vow he had sat around in his apartment for two days. The problem was that he hadn't felt the rush of energy that he had felt in the past after completing the vow. Normally, after undertaking such a thing, he would be flooded with inspiration. Not so this time. It had been all he could do to go to Sapik's today, and he didn't even know if once he got home with the powder, he would have the will to clean. He stood at a corner one block away from Sapik's and one block away from his house. The sun was heating up the wind that was blowing around and bumping into things. A tough-looking tree dropped an object, some kind of seed or nut. The tree was the survivor of hundreds of staples, most of which had been used to post flyers for events that were boring, loud, and stupid. He noticed a cigarette butt that had been deliberately stuck into a piece of gum on the ground. Who bothered to do that? Why didn't they just flick it somewhere? He kept walking.

As he neared his building an idea came to Belkin.

He turned around and walked quickly back to Sapik's. He became more excited as he went. He realized that this idea was the first fruit of the Prometheus Vow.

"Sapik!" Belkin shouted from halfway through the door of the liquor store.

"Oh, the language scholar. Yes?"

"The reason I know about Cave Urdu is because my father studied it during the Cold War!"

"Oh. Haha, how odd. He must be have been a very bored man," Sapik said ironically.

"Not exactly . . . he's actually mentally ill. Anyway, listen. I want you to try to talk to him in Cave Urdu!"

"I don't understand."

"Goddamn it! What is there to understand? Why does everybody always have to understand everything? Why can't you just ask me for money or something? Why do we have to get in a discussion about this?"

Sapik looked wary. Roy remembered that people liked to become familiar with one another before getting to the point of whatever they were talking about. Belkin, on the other hand, liked to avoid familiarity and disallow even a single extra word. This put him at odds with strangers. *Slow down, Roy. Don't blow this, you fucking asshole*, he thought to himself.

He tried again with Sapik, in more measured speech. "My father has problems. He is . . . abnormal. I have trouble getting through to him. But he has an obsession with obscure languages, even though he speaks English. I feel that maybe, if somebody spoke to him in one of these languages, like Iroquois or, well, like Cave Urdu, he might respond."

Sapik looked at Roy carefully from behind the counter. The store was quiet. The door tone chimed as another customer walked in, but Sapik didn't shift his gaze from Roy. He seemed to be making some kind of assessment.

"I'll do it," he said finally.

They arranged to go that afternoon. Sapik wouldn't accept any offer of money. Roy rushed home, more optimistic than he had been in years.

His plan was not designed to create personal communication with his father. He had given up on that idea years ago. What he wanted was help with the Balfour case. Ulmers Belkin was, after all, a genius. And what was the Pernice Balfour situation if not a code? Here we had a perceived set of events that represented another set of events. Pernice Balfour as a murdering arsonist was a kind of cipher for what really happened, whatever that was. It seemed to Roy that his father's powers of decryption might help untangle it. Since Ulmers had a fetish for obscure languages, hearing Cave Urdu might pique his interest enough that Roy could get a question through. Roy knew it was a long shot, but it was an inspired one.

At three o'clock he rejoined Sapik at the liquor store. A somber-faced, younger man had taken over behind the counter. Sapik was waiting outside when Belkin got there.

"Okay. You ready?" He asked.

"Yes," Sapik responded.

They started to walk down the street. Belkin was nervous. At first he had been excited about the idea but he had come up with some doubts. The problem was that he wasn't sure if it would work. Also he would have to spend a long time riding the bus with Sapik. He liked the man; he just was no good at manufacturing conversation. He had prelisted this threat on the Shield:

22. SPEECH NOTHINGNESS ON BUS WITH LIQUOR STORE CLERK

Fortunately Sapik passed the time during the bus ride by telling Roy about Cave Urdu.

"It was created by ancient holy men around Northern India. Uninformed Western linguists named the dialect 'Cave Urdu' because they thought that the ascetics who spoke it lived in caves and it was a variation of the Urdu language. Actually, though, the ascetics who created it did not live in caves and it isn't Urdu at all. It was created by a small group of Sadhus who were kicked out of the caves because the others didn't like them. In protest for being kicked out they eliminated all hard consonants from their speech, which is one of the reasons it is so difficult to learn."

"Hmm," Belkin said.

"Also it is called a reactive or transliterate language because it is entirely based on a set of memorized parables in another tongue. They speak only in parables."

"Wait, what?" Belkin asked.

"Oh you know, like stories, religious instruction. The inventors of Cave Urdu took a set of one hundred religious parables and replaced every word. That is the basis of the language and how they instructed newcomers in it."

"So can you talk about other things besides these parables? I mean, I was hoping to ask my father about something."

"Hmm," Sapik answered. "Maybe."

Belkin dug his fist into the seat.

"But if your father knows the language well, we can definitely exchange unique variations of the dialogue related to the parables," he assured.

"That's not exactly what I was hoping for."

The rest of the bus ride was silent until just before they got to the stop. Then Belkin turned to Sapik. "Why are you studying it anyway?"

"I have an uncle who speaks it," Sapik answered. "If you want to know the absolute truth, he has a lot of money and I am trying to win favor with him."

"That's sensible."

The walk to his father's apartment was short. When they got to it, Agent Hoose wasn't there. Ms. Calbenza opened the door for Roy and Sapik.

"Roy! The heaven blessed a lot today! Dumped a nice blessing."

"Thank you, Ms. Calbenza. This is Sapik. He is going to try to talk to my father."

"Roy, you know that am not easy!"

"Well, I know."

"Roy, you are a heaven!"

"Thanks, Ms. Calbenza."

"You go ahead, he are in there!"

They went into the living room. Ulmers was there at the pile of computers. He looked especially deep in the weeds. His face was white and his head seemed to be crackling with static electricity. Belkin didn't say anything. Sapik looked at the old man and then at Belkin quizzically.

"Oh, there's no point in introducing you. He's completely out of it. You may as well just charge right ahead with the Cave Urdu. Try to make it loud. Think of yourself as trying to penetrate the wall of a tornado or something."

Sapik gave Belkin the same look of assessment that he had given him in the store when Belkin first asked if he would come with him. Suspicious but curious. Then he turned to Ulmers.

"RAAAAAOOOORRREEEOOOOAAAUUUUUUUH!"

Ulmers looked up from his work. He looked surprised for only

a moment. Then he closed his eyes. After a few seconds of searching he opened them and looked directly at Sapik.

"*OOOOHHHHHAAAAAAA-UH-UH-UH-OHHHHH-
AAAAY!*" he shouted back with relish.

Roy nearly fell on the floor. Sapik and Ulmers started moaning
and shrieking back and forth like a pair of cheerful hyenas. Belkin
interjected after a few minutes.

"What are you two talking about?"

Sapik was red in the face and out of breath. "We were recount-
ing the dialogue about how the snake lost his wings."

"Sapik! Listen: tell him that I have a friend who was set up for
a murder! How should I go about clearing her name?"

"What?"

"I need to know how to clear the name of a friend who has
been falsely accused!" Belkin gave Sapik a brief rundown of the
Pernice Balfour situation.

"Well," Sapik responded, "there is a parable about a tiger that
gets accused of eating a fox. Maybe I could ask him in those
terms."

Sapik turned to Ulmers.

More moaning and shrieking ensued. Belkin noticed an open
window in the living room. There was a crow outside on a telephone wire. The crow seemed to be taking no notice of the odd
noises. *Isn't it strange how much more dignified animals are
than people,* he thought.

After a few more minutes Sapik turned to Belkin.

"Well, he said that you must go to the fox's den."

"He said that? About my friend? I mean, he came up with that
idea?"

"Not exactly. Really it's just how the parable goes. These exchanges are somewhat scripted. In the story, that was how the tiger ended up clearing his name. He goes to the den of the fox that everybody thinks he ate and establishes his innocence. These parables are all written by religious devotees. The story is a metaphor for giving up the sense of guilt one accumulates over being caught in the wheel of karma. Nonetheless, it was your father's response."

"All right. Well, I suppose that's close enough."

"Do you mind if your father and I finish the parable before we leave? This is the first time I've actually been able to practice with another person."

Sapik and Ulmers continued shouting at each other until the conclusion of the exchange. When it was done, Ulmers turned and dipped back into the world of his electronic project as if he had never been interrupted. Belkin and Sapik stood there and watched him for a few more moments.

"It's very strange," Sapik said, watching Ulmers Belkin retreat into his inner world.

"Well, it's not so odd, really. I mean, who really listens to each other anyway?"

"Most people are fully capable of interacting with others," Sapik said.

"They are? I always thought they were mostly just making social noises and focusing on their own instinctual pulls."

"Why would you say that?"

"I don't know. I suppose I'm not very well-adjusted. Look at my father."

"Ahh," Sapik said.

On the bus ride back neither of them said anything. People got on and off the bus. The bell rang for stops. The bus driver was screened from the view of passengers but Belkin saw his arm emerging from behind the plastic partition to accept bus transfers. The partition was black. Belkin sleepily relaxed his gaze. Now the driver's area looked like an ominous black square floating in the air with a meaty arm that emerged every so often to accept a bus transfer. Afterward the arm would sink back into the black square.

When they got back to Belkin's apartment he skipped his stop so that he could go to the next one and get off the bus with Sapik. They stood outside the liquor store.

"You sure I can't give you a few bucks? At least for your time?" Belkin asked.

"No, that's all right," Sapik responded.

"Well, thanks. You've helped me quite a bit."

"You're welcome. I hope you find a way to talk to him someday. It is very important to get along with your parents, you know."

"It is?"

"Yes! Of course!"

"Oh."

Sapik gave him the inquisitive look again. Then he shook Roy's hand and went into his store.

Belkin walked home. He felt optimistic. His plan had worked. "Go to the fox's den," his father had said. The fox in the story had been killed. Obviously this meant he should go to Frank Relpher's apartment and poke around. A quick scan of remembered detective media confirmed that this was the right action. The idea was to be at the crime scene with a flashlight, according to how the stories went. Of course his father hadn't directly thought about the problem, or even thought about it indirectly for that matter. With Ulmers Belkin, it was more like reading tea leaves than having normal communication, Roy decided. You had to take what information you could get.

Belkin stood outside the door of Frank Relpher's apartment. It was the night following Sapik's and his visit to his father.

The whole floor that the burned flat was on was under reconstruction because of water and smoke damage. The apartment was on the seventh flour, four stories above his own. The door to Relpher's apartment was partially burned. There were two brightly colored paper seals on the door as well as a plastic device that was screwed to the wall and held the door closed. The plastic device said SECUR-LOC on it. Belkin gave the door a flaccid kick. A piece of the frame ripped out and swung inward with the door, still attached to the undamaged police locking device. The molding had been weakened by the fire.

The room smelled of soot and chemicals. He didn't know if the chemical smell was from what had been used to start the fire or to put it out. He shined his flashlight around.

The interior was cluttered. Plumbing equipment, locks, hundreds of small pieces of pipe, hooks, screws, beaten-up toolboxes, and other stuff covered the floor. The apartment looked like a hardware store that had been shaken up and then reorganized in wild piles. Belkin made the man's bed out amid the clutter. It was nothing more than a gray mattress. He then saw what must have been the fire's point of origin, a large area of blackened debris in one corner. The pile consisted of burned wood, pipes, wires, and other things, as though somebody had assembled a mass of junk, some of it flammable and some not, dumped gasoline on the whole mess, and lit it. This area was cordoned off with blue string. Various points within the stringed-off area had plastic evidence markers with numbers on them. Relpher's body would have been lying on that pile of junk and the killer must have dumped the chemicals right on top of him, Belkin surmised. The rest of the apartment was burned, but not completely. He tried to imagine what a *clue* would look like as he passed his beam over all the wreckage. He couldn't get over how much junk the man left lying around.

He wandered around a bit more, not really sure what to look for. He had to step carefully. An entire wall was lined with cans of paint, shellac, varnish, spackle, and other products. An enormous box was filled with lengths of wire of every variety. Bags of plumbing parts leaned against bags of other stuff. Belkin recognized the state of Relpher's apartment as the final triumph of the Slow Evil. After a while he carefully stepped back through all the debris and made his way out the door. He hadn't discovered anything in particular.

He went to sleep that night wondering if he had accomplished anything and was now full of anxiety from seeing the dead man's apartment. The place felt like a grave, but not because it was a murder scene. Belkin was sure that the bleak, merciless atmosphere would have been worse *before* the fire had occurred. If anything, torching some of that crap probably cheered it up. After a while Belkin slumped into a kind of sleep where he rifled through deep, bad thoughts rather than dreaming.

He slept late the next day. When he woke up he noticed that an envelope had been slid under his apartment door. There was a note in it.

Dear Mr. Belkin,

This is Emile LeCroix, the crime scene photographer that you met at the police station when you went to speak to Detective Morpello. I got your address from the interview documents. I thought you might be interested in the following. The other day I was taking a few extra photos and I asked the landlord of your building if there was a dark area in the building where I could change a roll of film. You see Roy, I still use the old-fashioned cameras. Anyway, he gave me a key to the basement. While down there I poked around a bit and discovered that Frank Relpher had a small maintenance office back behind the main furnace. I don't think the landlord even knew about it. Anyway, I thought about telling Detective Morpello but then I remembered the amazing conversation you and I had at the police station the other day and thought if anybody should know about Relpher's "sanctum sanctorum" it should be Royal Belkin. I made a copy of the key before giving it back to the landlord. And the rest is up to you.

Joyously,

Emile LeCroix

There was a key in the envelope with the letter. Belkin tore up the note but he put the key in his pocket. *Royal* Belkin? That was the danger of making forays out into the streets; you could attract the human element of the city back to your safe zone. Now they were coming after him in his own apartment. Still, there was a new area to investigate. He would wait until that night.

For now he would get to work on the Service. You couldn't let the demands of the outside world ruin your personal work. You couldn't. You had to do what was important. You had to stick with what you did, even if moral or civic obligation called you away from time to time.

He sat down at his computer and found the Helping Hands website. He felt the usual enthusiasm. On this day he felt particularly inspired. On a normal day he would warm up with a few answers but today he started off with a question of his own.

Belkin127 asks: Have you heard of The Gospel of Lazarus?
Details: My therapist gave me a book about a gospel that was discovered in a desert in 1994. The book has new important facts:

1. Jesus could fly
2. He learned a lot of the things from a Chinaman
3. He could not wilk on water
4. He could heal people but only with bread, not with hand
5. He loved the lady from the well
6. He killed some people in Egypt which is why he was on the run
7. He was not a caprenter, more like magician or doctor
8. Some of them were gays
9. When he was in the desert he also fought a cobra
Do you agree

Undeserving answers: If you keep putting these asinine questions up you should at least change your name so that everybody doesn't simply know it's you over and over again.

Wheatfromthechaff answers: And you my friend are a liar! What makes you think anybody is going to believe your lies? I will pray for you.

LilJulie answers: There is no gospel of Lazarus only Mathew Mark Luke and John.

Belkin felt inspired by the Bible theme and continued.

Belkin127 asks: When Jesus killed the nun why did people still stand by him?
Details: My therapist told me that Jesus killed a nun using stones. First of all, why did he kill her and also if she was pregnatn how did he know it was his and also why did Paul and Jospehp still stick with him and think he was still the mezah.

GodsVictory answers: LOL my friend, you need to get rid of the therapist! Jesus never killed anybody! I recommend going right to the source: God's word. Try Mathew 5 to find out what His message was really about! Good luck and God Bless!

It went on for a while longer. After he was done there was still half a day to kill before it was late enough to go down to the basement. He looked in the kitchen cabinet and realized that it was time to go shopping. He had gone through a lot of supplies in the tub and in the days following. He wrote out his shopping list and then put on the Shield. The way he seemed to be running around the city lately he thought that maybe shopping would be easier than usual. He did his habitual internal check to see how bad the Pounding of the outside world was. It was at level 7. He felt the usual fear as he forced himself out the door. One of Belkin's mottos was "The Pounding can reach you."

This admonition was borne out as soon as he stepped out of his apartment. There in the hall was the blue bag of filth that one of his neighbors liked to leave out every week. Anger and fear came. He looked at the door with the bag sitting outside of it. It was across the hall from his apartment and down a few feet. The tenant in that apartment had a baby in there—already an outrage. This person added to the problem by subscribing to some kind of "diaper service" and leaving the bags out every week to be collected. Presumably the bags contained soiled cloth diapers—a thought so disgusting that Belkin immediately tried to put it out of his mind. He had already left three notes on yellow pieces of paper stuck to the baby owner's door:

(Monday, December 28):
This is filth. —A neighbor

(Monday, January 4):
Filth. —A neighbor

(Monday, January 11):
To leave filth is to BE filth. —A neighbor

He went back into his apartment and got out the yellow pad. He would have to be a bit stronger, he thought.

DO I HAVE TO WRITE THIS NOTE IN SHIT FOR YOU TO UNDERSTAND? —A NEIGHBOR

Satisfied, he stuck the note on the person's door and began his trip to the supermarket.

Once there he ended up with more or less the same assemblage of goods that he always ended up with: several olive-based products, some vegetables, canned potatoes, cashews, sponges, canned shallows fish, peasant bread, disinfectant, parsley, Melba toast, condensed milk, bismuth, lava soap, yogurt, lemons, jicama, mixed bitters, and rock cheese. He felt the Shield underneath his shirt and avoided looking at anybody. He made it home with the items.

💬

Night enveloped the city as usual. Before long it was 1:00 AM and Belkin took the elevator down to the lobby of his building. The basement door was off the lobby. The key that LeCroix had slid under his door in the envelope worked. He went down a flight of steps into the darkness with his flashlight. The dim beam shined around the room. It was grim. The walls were dark gray and there was dust and subterranean grime everywhere. It was cold and things echoed. He saw a large tank with ducts coming off of it. That must be the main furnace that LeCroix referred to in his note. He walked around it. There in a corner, enclosed by pipes and piles of cardboard boxes, was a small den-like area. There was a desk with a shabby lamp and a rack with some tools affixed to it. Not much of an office really, just an improvised area in which one could make notations in logbooks and screw things together, Belkin thought, trying to imagine what exactly a maintenance man did. Even so, this little area had the same bleak vibrations that Relpher's apartment did. The whole space, as small as it was, was filled with boxes and piles of junk.

There was something sorrowful and lost about this man Relpher. It was amazing how the emotional aura of a person infected his surroundings. Maybe when Belkin was up in his apartment fighting the Slow Evil, he was actually just fighting the natural outgrowth of his own internal rot. *Maybe?* he thought. *As if there was any doubt.* Then he noticed that on the desk, beneath an old tool belt, there was a large manila envelope.

He reached for it. He tucked the flashlight under his arm in order to free his hands to look in the envelope. Inside there were photographs. He glanced around the dank basement. He could see why that weirdo LeCroix found this corner to change his film. It was pitch dark except for Belkin's sickly flashlight beam. He felt very little fear though. It was the daylight that scared him, not the darkness.

The photos in the envelope were of two naked people engaging in various sexual acts. *What kind of an animal was this "Relpher"?* he thought to himself. Then a realization began to break through into his consciousness that was so jarring that he almost couldn't get his mind to hold on to it. He flipped through the photos more desperately. There was no denying it. He felt weak and wondered if this is when one was supposed to sit down, to take the news sitting down, to deny the news, to suspect a cruel joke, to run, to rewind the tape, to commit suicide, to scream . . . the woman in the photographs was Pernice! It was some awful man and Pernice Balfour! The man in the photos was young, muscular, and nauseatingly virile.

Just as Belkin thought he simply couldn't take one more thing, he heard a footfall and saw a series of flashes in rapid succession. What now? He was off-balance, staggering from both the shock of the photographs and the violent bursts of light. His flashlight landed on the cement floor, went out, and rolled away. The flashes kept coming. He found the desk with one hand. In between the strikes of light there was total darkness. He remembered that there was a lamp on the desk and groped for it. After a bit of fumbling, it came on, and there was Emile LeCroix shooting pictures of him.

"Hello, Roy Belkin!"

"Stop it! What's wrong with you? Can't you see that this is the scene of an atrocity?"

"Just as I suspected. I knew that you would come here eventually," LeCroix responded.

"Why shouldn't I? You gave me the key!"

"Oh really?"

"Yes, of course!"

"Hmm. Maybe so. But why were you so intent on digging around anyway?"

"I'm trying to clear Pernice Balfour, that's why!"

"It looks to me as though you have just done the opposite!"

"I haven't done anything!"

"My friend, those obscene photographs you hold provide the police with the one thing they are missing in this case: motive."

"Well, I don't know anything about that. I just found these things . . . I still can't believe it."

Belkin sat down in resignation. The turn of events was overwhelming. He couldn't understand what this LeCroix was up to.

LeCroix smiled coyly. He stood there with his weight on one foot. He was short and shiny. His black curly hair seemed to be piled higher than it was on the first day Belkin had met him. "I found those photographs in here the other day," LeCroix said. "I left them in a more obvious place than I found them naturally, to bait the trap."

"The trap?"

"Yes, Roy Belkin. I knew you would come down here, given a little hint. What it is that you really want, I don't know and actually I don't care. It seems to me very likely that *you* were the one that killed Frank Relpher for your little girlfriend. And now you're just looking to clean up the mess."

"What?!"

"Never mind. As I said, I don't care. But I have photographs of you looking at the obscene photos of those two. That could lead the police in any number of directions, the very least of which is a guilty verdict for your young saint."

"Why are you telling me this? What is this? Who are you?"

"Mr. Belkin, there is something that I want from you. In exchange, I will turn over the film in this camera to you on this very night."

"What could you possibly want from me?" Belkin looked at LeCroix more closely as he asked him the question. LeCroix was wearing a plastic bow tie.

"Well, we both know that you are an unusual man. Full of a kind of raw sexuality that is almost forgotten in this world."

"What?" Belkin shouted. He felt as though if anything else happened, he might simply lose his mind on the spot, if he hadn't already. This LeCroix kept saying one amazingly misguided thing after another.

"Please, don't play modest with me. There is no time," LeCroix added.

"You're a lunatic!"

"Mr. Belkin, if you will consent to a photo shoot, I will turn over the film that I just shot of you."

"What kind of photo shoot?"

"Hmm . . . indeed," LeCroix mused. "Something not too contrived . . . above all, your energy is animalistic, dark, frightening . . . maybe we could do something right here . . . "

"Wait—are you a *homosexualist*?"

LeCroix squinted. "No . . . I suppose that I am a *Pan*sexualist. And I mean *Pan* in the mythological sense."

Belkin almost ran out of the basement, but he was held in place by the memory of the Prometheus Vow. Always, when one took an oath, circumstances would arise in resistance to the stated objective. The turbulence usually came about quickly and with great strength, as if to test one's resolve. Belkin identified the appearance of LeCroix as this discord in the universe, a natural counterforce to his push forward, the guardian at the gate. LeCroix was fumbling with a small, paint-spattered radio that was in the pile of junk next to the desk. He had it plugged in and was fishing around with the tuner. Belkin stood near him. After searching for a little while LeCroix landed on a radio station that was playing a song with a monotonous electronic beat. He turned up the volume. The speakers crackled and sputtered. The sound was deeply irritating.

"Okay, go ahead and strip!"

"This is going too far, LeCroix!" Belkin shouted over the music.

"Don't waste my time, Roy Belkin! Off with the clothes! Otherwise I'm sending your holy virgin straight to hell!"

"There's no way I'll do this!"

"Come on! It will only take a minute! Don't blame me for the fact that you have a gift. I'm only trying to bring it out! I'll shoot my photos and this will all be over!"

"Goddamn you!" Belkin shouted and undressed awkwardly.

"Ah there . . . yes!" LeCroix replied and eagerly rewound his camera. The music blasted away. A vocal track came on. It was distorted because of the strain on the battered speakers, but Belkin could make out the repeated phrase droning over the dance track.

I call it a feeling, I call it a feeling, I call it a feeling, I call it a feeling, I call it a feeling, I call it a feeling, I call it a feeling . . .

"Move for me, Roy! Just go with your energy! Dance it!"

Belkin began waving his arms stiffly. He was standing in his pile of clothing. The camera began flashing.

"That's it! Yes! Yes!"

The flashes kept coming, as did the music. Belkin jerked around angrily.

"You are a real fucking asshole, LeCroix!"

"That's it! Turn around! Let me see your stone!"

"Ugh! What is wrong with you? Why? Why?" Belkin turned around, now facing away from LeCroix, and tried to keep moving one way or another. He would vindicate Pernice. He would walk through all the blows. A vow was a vow. This man LeCroix was merely a phase of opposition.

"Yes, Roy! Make it smoke! *Show me some bastard!*"

Belkin remained turned away from LeCroix. The flashes were making him dizzy. Facing the wall he managed to see the activity as only physical. He rolled his head around and took small steps this way and that.

"Yes! I have been looking for you my whole life, Roy Belkin! Unleash your oil!"

"Disgusting! That's enough! I won't do this any longer!"

"Don't give me that," LeCroix chided, flashing away with the camera. "You're almost breaking new ground here! I'm getting incredible photos, brother! Try to do more with your pig!"

Belkin was getting out of breath. "Listen, LeCroix, I've met some real scum since I've been on this case, but you are the worst—the lowest piece of human shit I've ever seen!"

The flashes had stopped but the music continued to blare out of the cheap radio. The song seemed to last forever.

"SHAKE YOUR SACK! UNGGG! UNGG! ARRRGGGH!" LeCroix shouted.

"All right, that's it!" Belkin shouted, turning around. "My God! What are you doing! You didn't say you were going to do that!" he screamed at LeCroix.

"UNGGGGGGGG!"

"Stop it! Stop!"

"AAAAHHHRRR . . . ungh aaah . . . "

LeCroix sat on the floor. Belkin turned off the radio and leaned against the desk. He wanted to throw up, if only to make a point, but he couldn't.

"Well, that was fantastic. Are you happy now?" Belkin asked.

LeCroix slumped his shoulders. His face was covered with sweat. The camera hung limply around his neck.

"Actually, I feel a little let down."

"Give me the film, LeCroix!"

"I mean, here I've just had the great sensual experience of my life." He sighed. "I managed to *gunk*, a rare pleasure. Your dance—it more than met my expectations. It was what I thought I had been looking for all these years . . . and where am I now? Or maybe I should ask, *who* am I now?"

"LeCroix, if you don't give me the film, I'm going to kill you," Belkin said.

"Oh . . . don't worry Roy, there's no film in the camera."

"I saw it flashing! Give me the film, LeCroix. I did your ridiculous 'dance'!"

"Here, I'll show you." LeCroix got up and opened the back of the camera. There was no film in it. "You see, you don't need film to operate the flash," he said, and he activated the flash a couple of times to demonstrate.

"Then why did you do this?"

"*L'expérience érotique*. It's the drama of the imagined blackmail that makes our little dance forbidden. But after one has transgressed, *escaped from the chapel*, as it were, it seems that he is more trapped than ever before—a kind of imprisonment that only a man who has had a glimpse of the sun can imagine—the great disappointment of knowing that one must always return to his cell," he said despondently.

Belkin got dressed. He was tired, tired.

"You are looking for something, Belkin . . . I was looking for something I thought I had found in you . . . but beware of finding it. It may be that the only emancipation there is lies in the dream of some diamond of the future . . . the longing . . . "

"Is everybody in the world insane?!" Belkin said, and he walked up the long flight of stairs leading back to the lobby.

"Farewell! And thank you!" Lecroix said from below as Belkin ascended.

He had the pornographic photos of Pernice Balfour tucked under his arm. The flashes from LeCroix's camera were imprinted on his eyes in spots that floated around his gaze. If only he had worn the Shield! He had put LeCroix on it! But the Shield had been designed for excursions outside the building. Clearly the Pounding could reach all the way into the home.

9.

The next day Belkin waited in the reception area of jail number 8 with nothing going through his mind. The reason for his blankness was that he hadn't slept. Emotions were drained out of him, as were thoughts. Those had been expended last night in a long, hot cycle of going over and over the horror of his disillusionment. Now all there was was mute apathy. The visiting protocol for Pernice had been changed for some reason. This time they had to talk through a partition.

"Lordly Blessings, Roy!" she whispered.

"Don't give me that shit, Balfour!"

"Belkin, in the name of Lord . . . "

"What is this? What is this?" he said, waving the photographs of her in front of the Plexiglas.

"Where did you get those?!" she screamed.

"I found them in Frank Relpher's sanctum sanctorum."

"Oh, Detective Belkin! I'm so sorry!" Pernice said.

She's just like all the rest of them, Belkin thought to himself, although he had actually met very few women in his life. He sat there watching her through the Plexiglas.

"You see, Roy, how I was before LORD?"

"But you've been omitting things and covering your tracks. That was after Lord."

"It's the shame!"

"Mmm."

"Detective Belkin, please stay on the case!" Her face was melting and sloshing against the barrier. Belkin's face was drawn forward as if being sucked into the lava.

"No!"

"Please, Mr. Belkin!"

"All right."

"I'll tell you everything I know! I won't leave out anything, I promise! Why didn't you visit on the last visitation day?"

"I was doing some tub-work."

"Well, Detective, I didn't omit anything really. I mean those photographs don't have anything to do with Frank Relpher or any of this."

"They don't? What was he doing with them?"

"He just stole them from an album in my apartment, along with the other photographs that the police found in his apartment, that I already told you about," she said.

"I have met a lot of filth, a lot of scum on this case. I didn't know that you were one of them. I'm going to stay on it because I made a vow that almost killed me. But let me just ask you something about this . . . this act of depravity." Belkin pointed at the photos without looking at them. "Did somebody blackmail you into doing this? That I could understand."

"No—it was my idea. That fellow in the pictures was just a guy I knew from an old job I used to have at a car dealership. I always wanted to explore my dramatic side, so we shot those one night after work. We used a camera with a timer."

"Oh."

"But I'm not that way anymore! Since Lord, my bread is Bible, not flesh! Not fleshly bread! Word bread! Lord's word!"

Belkin squeezed his leg so hard that his fingers almost ripped through his pants.

"Tell me whatever else you may have left out. Hurry up! We're short on time here."

"I thought about it the last couple of days. The only thing I could remember that I hadn't told you was that Frank threatened me. He said, 'I'm going to ruin your life.'"

"Ruin your life?"

"Maybe he planned to do something with those pictures," she said. "He said that to me about a month after I broke things off. I ran into him in the hallway. He was going somewhere. You know, just doing some building stuff, I guess. And he said, 'You ruined my life and now I'm going to ruin your life.'"

"What else?"

"He didn't say anything else."

"What other details can you give me?"

"That's all I remember. After Father Basil talked to him he never bothered me again, except for that one time that I just told you about."

"Nothing else when you were seeing him? Did he know anybody? Did he seem involved with anything? Phone calls? Anything?"

"Nope. We just went and had a few hamburgers and went to the movies once and then after that I cut him off. To tell you the truth, I never really wanted to go out with him in the first place, but I was lonely and bored and he pressed the issue."

"Hmm."

"Detective Belkin, I'm sorry about the sin of omission I hath committed."

"Forget it. Seeing those pictures didn't change anything. It just made everything go back to the way it was before."

"Before what?"

Belkin didn't know the answer. "Well, let me ask you this: are you going to stop lying or not?"

"Yea verily, I hath not lied since I told the falsehood unto the police."

"One more question: I don't suppose you have an alibi for when the murder took place?"

"No. I was alone in my apartment."

"Great. Well, that's the way things are going lately."

"I'm sorry."

The irony of Pernice expressing sympathy to Belkin for her own misfortune was lost on her. That was the kind of guilelessness that had won Belkin over from the start. As he looked at her he wondered how she could so easily shoot those sex photos. People were complicated. Actually, they were simple. The complicated part was in trying to understand them. A few more minutes went by and then the visiting period was over.

On the cab ride home Belkin wondered why he was so prudish anyway. He had been raised by Ms. Calbenza, who was a religious fanatic, but he never took anything she said too seriously. Still, he found all forms of sex revolting. He saw it as a kind of feral possession. He fought it in himself and reviled it in others. The cab shouldered its way through the downtown traffic. He saw an enormous billboard in Union Square that seemed to confirm his feelings. It showed a close-up of man and woman's midsections. The models were clothed. You couldn't see their faces, only their groins. Both were wearing partially unzipped jeans. Under the name of the clothing brand was the slogan "People Need People."

When Belkin got home it was two o'clock in the afternoon. He felt as if he hadn't slept properly in weeks as he opened the door to his apartment. There on the floor was an envelope. He groaned and picked it up. He poured cold coffee into a cup and took the envelope over to the small table he had by the window. It was from LeCroix.

Dear Roy,

Thanks again for the photo shoot the other night. Thank you. Was it last night? Things recede into the past so quickly, one wonders if they were merely dreams.

I am writing this note to let you know that when I first went down to the basement and found the compromising photos of Miss Balfour that are now in your possession, I also found another photo. The other photo is of Frank Relpher. As far as I know, it is the only one that exists aside from his driver's license.

I am enclosing it. I believe that you didn't have anything to do with the killing of Frank Relpher and that you are honestly just trying to help your friend Pernice. How do I know this? You showed me more than you realize in your dance. If I didn't tell you before, it was wonderful (the dance).

Anyway, feeling a bit depressed today. My mother is in town which is always like being in the presence of toxic waste. We will probably go up to the Top of the Mark this afternoon so that she can get drunk and call it "sight-seeing." If she starts crying and talking about my sister (who is now officially, literally, a whore, but that's another story) you may have another murder on your hands, this time a matricide! Actually I hope she does get drunk because then she will go to sleep early and I can have some darkroom time. I still haven't made proof sheets from the holidays! I also wanted to go shopping this week for pants but now that's out of the question. Oh well. Good luck with your case and I hope to see you again soon.

> *Pleasurably,*
> *Emile LeCroix*

He crumpled up the note and threw it against the wall. There was a photograph in the envelope. He looked at it. It was black and white. In it, Frank Relpher sat on a toilet in a bathroom stall.

The man was overweight, in his forties, and ugly. He looked like one of the guys you would see in a boxing ring corner squirting water into a prizefighter's mouth. His eyes were tired and empty. One of his hands hung in front of his knee. The hand was meaty. On the photo, written in permanent ink, were the words GOTCHA! SORRY FRANK! 1996. Relpher must have had one friend, Belkin thought. Or at least an acquaintance that knew him well enough to surprise him in the bathroom. Belkin looked at the photograph closely. Frank Relpher had thinning brown hair and a head like a roasted ham. Oddly, one of his legs was all the way out of his pants. As with Relpher's apartment, the man himself suggested death somehow. Here was a normal, overweight man, the type of guy who would be forgotten by the city, who would eat unhealthily, who would have an unhappy family and die a semianonymous death, and yet there was a greater-than-normal darkness about him. It wasn't that he had stolen photographs from Pernice, nor that he had a problem with household clutter, or even that he looked unhappy—it was something else. The way that Belkin felt when he had "investigated" the apartment and the way that he felt now when he looked at the photograph told him that he was dealing with an unusually bleak consciousness. Part of this impression was caused by the fact that in the photograph Relpher was being surprised and yet his face registered no emotion.

He continued to look at the picture as he thought about the greater problem. How could he find out more about this guy? Who had met Frank Relpher? Pernice and . . . *the priest*. Pernice had mentioned her problem with Relpher to the priest at her work, who had subsequently gone and talked to him. He sighed in frustration, knowing there was nothing to do but go see the priest.

On the street he clutched at the Shield beneath his shirt as if holding it were preventing him from being blown away. The endless trips out of the house were really starting to drag him down. He didn't feel that it was doing him good to get out of his shell. He felt that his shell did him good and that the less he saw of the city and of humanity the better. Pernice had said that this priest worked in a soup kitchen called Our Father's House. Belkin had looked it up. It was in the neighborhood.

He got to it. He walked through a storefront. Nobody was in the small dining room in front but there was some activity in a kitchen in back. There were two or three people cooking and washing dishes. A woman with gentle cow eyes and an oily nose sent him upstairs, where she said he could find Father Basil in his office.

The priest sat behind a desk in a room full of books, down a short hall from the stairway. He had very dark skin, almost black, and he spoke with a faint accent.

"I didn't know she was in jail. This is a terrible situation. I will visit her. Yes, she works here, but she drops in on a volunteer basis, so we didn't miss her," Father Basil said.

"I'm trying to clear her. This isn't easy for me but I have made a vow. I'm sure you can understand that sort of thing."

"I can understand," Father Basil said. "I met Relpher only briefly. He had developed a problem with Pernice, as you know. So I went and I talked to him."

"What did he say?" Belkin asked.

"I cannot tell you anything that was said."

"Can you tell me about him?"

"No."

Belkin sat there. The priest sat across from him. The room felt good, warm. The furnishings were all secondhand. This man Basil had an air of silence about him. There was no awkwardness in the lapses in talk. Instead, Belkin's thoughts just sank down into a nice level of sleepy mind-fuzz there in the modestly furnished room.

"You see, Roy, it is my job to make any person who talks to me feel as though they can say what they want to in confidence. The way that I do that is by not having conversations about other conversations."

"Mmmuuuhh," Belkin said fuzzily, lost in unexpected relaxation.

The priest looked at Belkin. Belkin sat there. He forgot why he was there or what he wanted to know. He wanted to sit there forever with this man whose aura seemed to clean out the poison.

"I don't believe in God," Belkin said. He didn't know why he said it.

Father Basil looked at Belkin and didn't say anything for a little while.

"Sometimes it's not as important to find God as it is to find what works," he finally answered, as if Belkin's statement was perfectly congruous.

"To find what works?"

"If you get up in the morning and you want to be alive more than you want to be dead, then you have found something that works."

"Oh."

"Have you found something like that?"

"No."

"Then it's important for you to know that this kind of thing exists for every individual, the possibility of meaning. I am a priest, but I must be honest with you, the possibility of meaning precedes religion."

"Oh," Belkin said.

"Of course I am a person of faith. It's just that often the first step is to have faith in life itself."

Again the room became silent. The silence hung in the air and then became the air, so that everything in the room including Father Basil and Belkin himself seemed to be suspended in the absence of noise. It was a strange sensation but not uncomfortable. They sat that way for twenty seconds. Father Basil leaned forward with his elbows on the desk and his fingers crossed in front of his mouth. He seemed to be no stranger to long pauses. When he spoke next, his words emerged from the emptiness of their own volition.

"When I was young I worked for a long time in Western Africa. In the place I worked, there are many people who are dead in their own bodies. Once you are in such a state, you can do anything. You wouldn't believe the things that people do when they are dead inside their own bodies—inhuman acts. It's a real shame. So you can see why I think meaning precedes everything, even faith. Some type of meaning. Because truthfully, there are religious fetishists, many who attain positions of power in the church, who are also dead in their own flesh. So I say to you, find something that is important to *you*. That is the first step for each of us. In my opinion. This is just my opinion."

"Mmm," Belkin said. Each mundane object he looked at

announced itself with piercing clarity, as if emerging from a haze. The priest's shoe, a book, a stain on the cheap rug that was on the floor beneath them. Before Belkin could respond in any way, the woman from downstairs rushed into the room and told Father Basil that the sink was flooding. He got up.

"I'm sorry, Roy, I have to go. I can't tell you a single thing about this man Relpher any more than I could tell anything to somebody who came asking about *you*. Please come back some time. I would love to talk to you, to hear more about your life. Good-bye."

Outside, Belkin sat at a bus-stop bench. After a moment he thought, *Why am I sitting here?* He was still in the warm pocket of the priest's emotional atmosphere. There was something about the man. He couldn't remember why he went there in the first place. To learn something about Relpher? He had learned nothing. Then an idea occurred to him. The concept was so plain and unobtrusive that he wasn't even surprised by it, even though it changed everything.

Who was Frank Relpher, the man with the dead face with one leg out of his pants? Frank Relpher was a loner, a man who broke into apartments and stole things, a man filled with strange darkness and anger, a man who made threats, an eccentric, a man who worked with tools and chemicals. How was he connected to the arsonist?

What if Frank Relpher *was* the arsonist? Maybe whoever had killed him had used implements that *belonged to Relpher*. There was no proof of it, but it seemed to fit.

Instead of helping matters, the revelation made everything else more confusing. Who killed Frank Relpher? Why did they set up Pernice? Or was Belkin wrong about Pernice? Did she kill Relpher after all and get informed on by somebody else? By whom? Were there two arsonists? Was Relpher killed by his partner in arson? Was the other arsonist . . . *Pernice?* He still believed in her innocence, but the way the picture was shifting he couldn't discount anything.

By the time he got home the reprieve from his anguish that the priest had provided had dissolved. In bed that night he worried about everything. Then he started thinking about the act of arson itself. He pictured setting fires in buildings—spilling trails of gasoline and lighting matches, stuffing newspaper under bedding, lighting bookshelves from the bottom and watching the flames climb upward—the images were strangely relaxing. First he pictured burning his own building, and then burning other buildings. Then he imagined only flames, burning the whole world and especially himself.

When he woke up the next day he felt as hopeless and lost as he did when he had first become curious about this whole matter. He remembered what Father Basil had said about finding something "that works." If you wake up and want to be alive more than you want to be dead, you have found something that *works.* He still hadn't found it.

10.

As he lay in bed trying to get himself to move, an envelope slid into his apartment from the hall. LeCroix! Belkin lunged for the door. By the time he had gone through the locks, LeCroix was already down the hall. He saw him just as he slipped into the elevator. He seemed to be running. Belkin ran out into the hall in his bathrobe and rushed for the elevator. The door was shut and the thing was descending by the time he got there. In the stairway the soles of his feet slapped against the concrete slabs.

He rushed down and made it to the lobby just as LeCroix was coming out.

"Royal Belkin! I just left you a note. I didn't want to bother you." LeCroix was not as short as usual, wearing shoes with large heels. He wore a sweater that looked as if it was made of some kind of netting. The camera was around his neck.

"Listen, LeCroix, I don't have time for games anymore. Pernice Balfour is in trouble. Actually, I'm not even so sure about her anymore to tell you the truth, but I want to follow this thing through. Do you understand?"

"What aplomb! Let's capture it on film, Belkin! One more photo shoot? The basement is right there." He covered his mouth conspiratorially as if discussing a mutual temptation.

"Forget it! I want your help. Can you find out what is in the evidence room for this case? What they took out of Relpher's apartment? I need to know more details about the man. I mean I'm starting to get some kind of feeling, some kind of idea"— Belkin lapsed, unsure why he was even telling LeCroix about his intuitions, and then pressed on—"but I don't know what. I need more information about Relpher. Something more. Something is missing."

LeCroix's eyes widened. He leaned in toward Belkin. He leaned too far, too close. Belkin was barely dressed. A man in a bathrobe had the right to a certain perimeter. Belkin stepped back.

"Your fever is contagious, brother," LeCroix whispered.

"Well? Do you have access to that kind of thing or not? Just a list of what they took out of there . . . or something."

"Oh, Roy Belkin, I can do much better than that." Even though he was wearing platform shoes LeCroix was standing on his toes and rubbing his palms against his legs. "I can go in that evidence room and photograph all of it, any time I want. And do you know what? I'll do it!"

"Thank you, LeCroix. And listen, there's no need for any more notes under my door."

"Don't be ridiculous, Roy! It's no bother, I'm happy to stay in touch."

"Well, I don't want you to stay in touch in that way."

"Hahaha! It's fine, *Royello*! I'll slip you another one soon. Heehee! Anyway, I'll photograph everything! Everything! Oh heehee!" LeCroix jogged through the lobby with his heels clacking against the linoleum and out the front door.

Back in his apartment, Belkin read the note that LeCroix had left.

Roy,

Emergency: I'm so bored! Listen, I am tired of crime scenes, dead bodies, and grouchy detectives! Help! Oh I'm just kidding. You are actually the only breath of fresh air I have going right now, far be it from me to ask you for more help. How are you doing?

Things are pretty good over here. My mother left (maybe God does exist!) and so now I am cleaning up the wreckage. Emotional, not physical. Although trying to get the smell of cigarette smoke out of my apartment does get a bit physical come to think of it. And no, I can't ask her not to smoke. Let me explain something Roy, my mother is not the type of person you want to ask to do anything. Here's why: once she knows what gets to you she will actually do it more. I'm not kidding about this one! You know, one of those people who if you want her to agree with you, you say the opposite of what you actually think. In other words, If I tell her not to smoke in my house I better stock up on extra ashtrays because she will show up with Havannah cigars as soon as I say it. Actually, I encourage her to smoke BION (Believe It Or Not). It might help her to "move things along" if you catch my drift. I would trade two weddings for a good funeral right now. OH I'M JOKING ROY BELKIN. Shame on you. LOL! Anyway, the good news is that's the last you'll hear about her for a while.

I might be going to L.A. for a couple of days this week so if you can't find me you can rest assured that I am PARTYING! My friend Aloys (No he didn't make that name up, You, he's Danish!) has gotten his "yacht" fixed. Well, Roy, that's what he calls it! LOL! What it really is a leaky-creaky houseboat with a vermin problem (not the least of which vermin is Aloys himself)! What is surprising is that he hosts some of the best parties in all of Hollyweird in that smelly old boat and you wouldn't believe the people that show up. Last time I was out there I drank schnapps with Jon Voight! I am not kidding. Wake me up when I'm dead!

> *Delighted,*
> *Emile LeCroix*

Belkin threw the note in his toilet and waited for it to become soggy enough to flush. As he stood there he wondered who he could talk to about his idea that Relpher was the arsonist. It now seemed like an important idea. But the investigation was being run by the imbecile Morpello. He would have to get around him. He couldn't imagine getting anything through to that man, no matter how simple it was. He went back to his table by the window. Now that he was getting out of the house more often he was getting a sense of how claustrophobic his surroundings truly were. He looked around the room. It was small and had very little furniture besides his desk, his single bed, a bookshelf, and his little table by the window where he drank cold coffee and ruminated.

Taking stock of his surroundings made him remember his personal work. *You can't give away all your time*, he thought to himself. He switched the computer on. For some reason on this day he was led to lash out at all the different spiritual paths rather than just focusing on Christianity. He normally stuck to what he knew but he was feeling expansive. As he worked he got hotter and hotter. The questions just started coming to him. He didn't have any time to answer other people's questions; all he could do was demand answers, typing the queries as fast as he could but still lagging behind the slew of words that was dumping forth from his subconscious mind:

Belkin142 asks: Attention people of the Jewish faith: Fellow Sanhedrin! How can I become more Jew?

Details: I have thrice rinsed my beard and sprinkled blood upon the bundle of figs. Also, I saw my brother looking at my wife and so I threw a rock at her. Finally, I counted to one hundred, skipping all the prime numbers and burning the shame candle. Is there anything I forgot?

Belkin142 asks: WICCANS ONLY: My name is Gwendolynia Goodwytche. I think that I have lost my power amulet!

Belkin142 asks: Mormons: I have been a Mormon for forty years.
I wanted to know once and for all, when Joseph Smith found the
Golden tablets near his Mule, were they a-buried in the earth or did
he have to go a-rootin' around for them in the shrubs? A-tell me thart!

Belkin 142 asks: Hindus only! I have summoned a fiery ape God and
I would like to civilize him. So far I have taught him to burn incense,
repair appliances and peel fruit. What I haven't taught him is to stop
shitting on the floor. Please help. Vishnu doesn't care and my landlord
is not a kindman, he is an angryman.

Belkin 142 asks: Children of the New Age: I am working on my affir-
mations. Are these good?
1. I am better than the others. The others will get diseases. I am a
Lord. They can all eat my shit.
2. I have a lot of Gold and no diseases because God is in my world.
The light of God is blasting forth from me and it gets rid of the weak
ones. The allergies are gone. I am a candle.
3. I am the king of all men. I am a great great man. The others are
stupid. I am sitting on my throne writing a kill list. Nobody will ever
defy me again. God is in my forehead. I am the light monster.
4. Golden nuggets are falling through my ceiling on to my floor where
I now collect them and cash them in so that I have the most power.
Fuck everybody, I am a rainbow.

Belkin142 asks: Muslims only please! I would like to give my wife
and the children some beating. My mouth is violent and I have oiled
the board. They are waiting for me. Should I cover my eyes for purity
before they takes off their tunics?

The words kept pouring forth. Suddenly he saw all the religions of the world as a single canopy, a grand staging area for his questions. The questions were truth. Truth was infinite and inexhaustible. The questions came out and found their own topics, going where they wanted to. The small personality called "Belkin" floated behind them as nothing more than a fragile memory, a name tag stuck to the larger reality of the Service.

Belkin142 asks: Buddhists only please!: I have reached a state of sheer boredom while meditating that has caused me to transcend everything and float effortlessly upon a cloud of total dullness. Can I go back to eating hamburgers now?

Belkin142 asks: Scientologists: I have seventeen human converts ready. Send the mothership to the usual coordinates. Zilgocktar. Avoid the thermoplasts. Travolta. Mog ook sot silzibeth. Clean the clean. Mentalizational interface. Don't accept any negatron.

It went on for about two hours and then stopped. By the time he was done the streak had cooled off and he managed to answer a few questions posted by other people and calm down. It was a prodigious day. Had it been the inspiration of meeting Father Basil? Or leftover mind-power from the tub ritual? Or was it just one of those things? It was impossible to know. Not that it mattered really. He got out his Thunder Journal, the book he reserved exclusively for miracles and disasters. The last entry he had written reminded him that it had been only two weeks since he had first met Pernice Balfour and become involved with her problems:

JAN. 14-
-THE DAY OF THE FIRE AND THE RELENTLESS
POUNDING.
-ENCOUNTERED "SHE."

It was remarkable how that single chance encounter had changed his life. Since then he had made more spontaneous trips out of the house and met more people than in a whole year previous. Whatever happened, he wouldn't forgive her for that, he resolved. Then he made a quick entry about his great afternoon.

FEB 5-
-INCREDIBLE SLEW OF QUESTIONS CAME TO ME
WHILE DOING THE SERVICE.

He put the journal away and shut off the computer. He felt like a moldy rag. He sat on his bed. What next? What was next? More investigation? It was a small, repetitive cycle of events that he lived in. When the phone rang an hour later he was still thinking about his problems but he hadn't come any closer to solving them. The weight of them pushed down on him. It was Pernice. For the first time he felt compelled to be totally honest with her.

"Detective Belkin! They let me talk to a lawyer and "I'm using her phone. I can only talk to you for a second. Have you made any progress?"

"Pernice, there's something I have to tell you."

"What is it?"

"I'm not a detective."

"What do you mean?"

"I lied to you. I'm just an ordinary person. Maybe even something lower than that, like a real fucking asshole. Actually, definitely."

"I don't believe it—really? Are you sure?"

"Absolutely. I'm sorry."

"Mr. Belkin, is this the truth?"

"Yes, it really is. There is definitely something wrong with me. I am not a detective. But I'm going to stay on the case."

"I can't believe it! I must pray."

"Again, I'm terribly sorry. To tell you the truth, Pernice, I've got a lot of strange habits and problems and apparently lying is one of them. But I never wanted to harm you in any way."

"LordLordLordLordLordLordLordLordLord . . . "

"Look, I'm going to stay on the case. I'm actually making progress."

"LORDLORDLORDLORDLORD . . . "

"For example, I think Relpher may have been the original arsonist. Does that mean anything to you? Does that trigger any connections?"

"Muhbuhguhbuhmuhbuhguhbuh . . . "

"Hello?" Belkin said.

"Muh buh guh bluh bluh muh guh bluh mubhuh glugjh..."

"Hello! I can't understand you at all!!"

"Muh buh guh bluh buh bluh guh muh buh gluglgoisdnf . . . "

"Pernice! I'm sorry about the lie! It was a terrible idea. I have to admit . . . I was trying to make an impression but it went too far!" Belkin shouted over Pernice.

She continued to make inarticulate noises.

Belkin hung up. He had obviously pushed Pernice over the edge with his goddamned lying. To make matters worse, not only had he lied to her, but here he was musing about how small his apartment was while she languished in a *cell* for God's sake. Even if she *was* guilty, maybe he could try to frame somebody else or something. He owed her that much. He got out the pad of paper on which he had made some initial notes regarding the investigation a couple of weeks ago. To these he added:

9. WHAT SHOULD I DO NEXT
10. I DON'T KNOW
11. NEED MORE CLUES
12. CRIME SCENE TOO DANGEROUS TO RETURN TO
13. SHOULD I GO BACK DOWN INTO THAT DIRTY BASEMENT?
14. YES I GUESS SO

It was bad news that he would have to return to that hellhole but Roy Belkin was a man of inner promptings. Once revealed, they couldn't be ignored. The truth was he had barely looked around down there before he was ambushed by Emile Lecroix. He would go back down to Relpher's creepy little maintenance den that night. He spent the rest of the day fighting the Slow Evil.

It was two in the morning. He went down to the lobby of his building and through the small door off to one side. This time he turned on a light in the basement rather than relying on his pathetic flashlight. He arrived at Relpher's little maintenance den and started going through junk. He went through the drawers of the small desk and also through the large drawers of an old file cabinet next to it. There were some steel tackle boxes that he emptied. All he found was more junk, tools, and hardware, the accessories related to building maintenance. What papers there were consisted of advertising circulars and occasional notes from tenants or from the landlord about problems that needed fixing. Belkin was meticulous about his search. After an hour he discovered something in a pile of sandpaper and pieces of linoleum. It was an address book. There were no addresses written in it, but clipped to one of the pages was a small bundle of receipts. The receipts were all from 1995. They were mostly records of purchases from hardware stores for the type of stuff that was scattered around the basement. As he went through the receipts he noticed a detail that was consistent with about half of them. There was a note at the bottom that said, "Bill to Rothgar Salvage account." He kept the receipts and then dug around for a while longer, fruitlessly. An hour and twenty minutes had passed. He ascended the steps of the basement and closed the door behind him.

In his apartment he looked up "Rothgar Salvage" on his computer. He found it on a resource site for electricians who rated parts stores.

●●●

Rothgar's Salvage

1347 Piedmont Street

San Francisco

Comments: This place sucks! Go here if you just want to pick through junk and get ripped off. They also have a lot of "hardware" which amounts to mostly garbage.

He turned off the computer and went to sleep.

11.

It was the next day. Belkin knew the correct busses to take. He poured a cup of cold coffee and drank it rapidly and then put on the Shield in preparation for yet another trip out into the heart of the Pounding. He ground his teeth together and performed much of his getting ready with his eyes shut.

He had the Shield on and he had the address of Rothgar's Salvage. He was ready to do more investigating. He opened the door of his apartment and walked out into the hall. He heard some low mumbling from the other end of the hallway. The passage was poorly lit as always but the two figures at the end of the long corridor of apartment doors were standing next to a light and so were discernible. Even from a distance he recognized the lumbering frame of detective Bud Morpello and another man. Belkin assumed that they were there to take a look around the building once again and he wondered if he should approach them with his latest thoughts on the subject of Frank Relpher. Down the hallway, Bud Morpello's arm raised slowly, pointing out Belkin to the other man. Belkin walked toward them. He didn't know who the other man was, but he thought that, unlike Morpello, he might be of at least seminormal intelligence, so it might be good to talk to them.

Belkin walked another fifteen feet before he realized that Morpello was pointing a gun at him. When Belkin heard the first shot he looked behind him to see if there was an attacker approaching. There wasn't anything but the rest of the hallway with its painted-shut window at the end. Then there was another shot. The report of the gun was like a punch in the head and it ended all other sound. Belkin wasn't hit but the shock was almost as if he had been. *My God, this idiot is firing a gun at me*, he thought as he turned and started running. The third explosion resounded from behind him as Belkin ducked into the stairway and ran down the stairs. Morpello was shooting at him! Why? He couldn't figure it out. He ran through the lobby and into the bright daylight with his ears still ringing from the gunshots.

Had Morpello thought Belkin was somebody else? Or was he trying to take Belkin out of the picture for some reason? Also, Belkin had written IDIOT DETECTIVE on the Shield more than a week ago. He was wearing the Shield. Why hadn't it worked?

Belkin quickly decided that going to the police about anything involving the case was out of the question. He was sure that Morpello had tried to kill him.

Rothgar's Salvage was many miles away in South San Francisco. South San Francisco is actually a separate city from San Francisco with an unimaginative name. Belkin had to take a bus and then the rapid transit train. The bus was terrible and the train was horrible. The whole trip was a ride through the nine phases of human squalor that constituted the Pounding: Crowding, Talk, Violence, Noise, Disease, Vapors, Commerce, Eye Contact, and Sweating. Over many years of suffering the Pounding, Belkin had come up with these categories. Having them itemized was no consolation.

After walking a few blocks from the train station, he arrived at a storefront in an industrial part of South San Francisco. The store was small but it had an adjoining lot filled with junk. There was a sign above the front window that read "ROTHGAR'S INDUS-TRIAL SALVAGE." In the window there was another sign that said "WE SPECIALIZE IN ELECTRONIC SCRAP." Beneath that sign was another one written in marker on the side of a brown grocery bag. This one was stuck to the window with duct tape and said "WE LOVE SWAPING. SHOW US WHAT YOU GOT." Belkin was still shaken from the attempted killing and tried to calm down before going in. He was determined to go forward with the investigation though it was getting dangerous. If a detective was after you, you were really in trouble, he feared. There was some consolation in the fact that Morpello was completely incompetent, almost catatonic. Belkin thought that he would probably see Morpello coming if he attacked again.

The lot on the side of the building elbowed into more lot in the back. Belkin stood in front of the whole entity. The sun was on the storefront with its big windows full of dusty junk. It made sense that Relpher had somehow been involved with this organization. The store and the lot were strewn with mechanical parts of every type and the place smacked of shell-shocked apathy. Among the various motors, small appliances, and pieces of electronic equipment there were out-of-place items like gardening supplies and stackable lawn chairs.

Inside, a man with a leaden beard was seated on a stool behind the counter. He was slender and had a face of iron dust and dog shit. Belkin greeted him and showed him the photograph of Frank Relpher, asking him if he looked familiar.

The man took the photo and held it up and laughed. Belkin marveled at the bleakness of the office.

"Ha! Where'd you get that? Sure I know him! Ha! Hey, Parmell! Haha! Come look at this!"

Another man emerged from the back. This man was black and built like a sack of potatoes.

"Haha! There he is! Where'd you get that?" the second man said.

"So you guys know Frank Relpher?" Belkin asked.

"Sure we do!" said the bearded one. "I took the photo! Frank used to work here. I'm Stan Rothgar. I hired him."

"Really? Can you tell me anything about him? What was he like?"

"Why do you ask?"

"He was killed. I'm an adjunct detective with the San Francisco Police Department."

Belkin ran down the story of the fire and the murder. Stan

Rothgar looked as if he were rusting on the spot. It was hard to tell whether he was listening or just sitting there stiffening up. Parmell laughed at everything.

These two are a real pair of dipshits, Belkin thought.

"Well, I can't say I'm sorry to hear he's dead. We had fun with him, but when it comes down to it, there was something wrong with that dude," said Rothgar through his red-gray beard.

"What do you mean?"

"Well, he ripped us off, for one thing."

"Now, you never proved that," Parmell countered.

"Oh, he was ripping us off all right."

"He was funny," Parmell said. "I'll tell you. This one time a lady came here and he locked her in the lot and left. She was out there in the lot in the rain. She had to ask somebody on the street to call us up. That was before cell phones, you know. They called and the phone rang in the office. Shit, we were all gone. Relpher locked the gate and went home. They had to have the police come and cut the lock. The lady was pregnant. She's lucky she saw somebody walking by."

"Do you know why he did it?" Belkin asked. He was trying to go with the prevailing tide of conversation, hoping it would lead to something useful.

At the question Parmell became thoughtful. "No, I don't," he said. "Frank said he just didn't notice her. I don't know if that's true. I don't see how he could have missed her."

"I'll tell you why he did it! Because he was a fucking asshole!" Rothgar said.

"What about this photo? What was going on here?" Belkin asked, holding it up again.

"Oh, we get bored around here. We used to try to get Relpher to show signs of life. You know, he was like a robot. We kicked in the door of the bathroom and shot that picture. We did other things too, like putting screws in his coffee and gluing things to his overalls. We never got a goddamn reaction out of him. It was like playing tricks on a big block of wood."

"He was taking a shit!" Parmell said. "When we took the photo! Haha!"

Rothgar got a smoky look in his eyes. His eyeballs rolled upward as if seeking a glance at the roof of his skull. He stuck his chin forward so that his beard was jutting forth.

"Uh-oh! Mr. Rothgar is about to start ranting and rambling, Detective."

"I'll tell you again, son," said Rothgar. He seemed as though he was going into some kind of trance. His was almost chanting as he spoke.

"I know what it means when he gets that look!" Parmell said excitedly.

"I didn't mean to upset you . . . " Belkin said. He turned and glanced at the front door of the shop behind him. Rothgar moaned under his breath and Belkin took a couple of halting steps backward.

"I'll tell you this again, my son," Rothgar repeated. His voice was rising, approaching the beginning stages of singing or wailing. "Frank Relpher waaaaaas a goddamned thief! A culprit of all a-sorts. From me he stooooole a solar calculator! From a-meee he a-stole seventy-two dollars! From a-me he a-stooooole 120 feet of a-copper wire! And I am not a lie. Ooooh no, I am not a lie!"

"Go ahead, Mr. Rothgar! Don't stop!" Parmell shouted. He was staring at his partner eagerly.

Belkin didn't know what to do except to pretend that Rothgar's episode wasn't happening. When Belkin spoke again he shouted and enunciated each consonant. "WELL—DID—YOU—FIRE—HIM—THEN?!"

He managed to break through.

"Oh no. We didn't figure out that he was stealing until after he left," Rothgar responded in his more conversational tone.

"Why did he leave?"

"He left because he went to jail," Rothgar said. "He got busted for breaking and entering. Turns out he was a burglar, I guess. Anyway, he only got six months. But he ended up doing four years! We were ready for him to get out six months later but he never got out. We got a postcard from him in '99. That was four years after he got busted. He wanted a job commitment, you know, to tell the parole board. Are you kidding? By that time . . . " Rothgar got the look again. "*By that . . . time . . . *"

"Uh-oh! Oh no!" Parmell said with glee.

"*By that time we a-knew! From meeeee he a-stole magazines! From meeeeee he a-stole paint! Even lunch meat! Riiight out of the a-fridgerator!*"

"What? What?" Parmell cheered.

"WHY DID HE END UP IN JAIL FOR FOUR YEARS?" Belkin shouted through.

"In-house violations."

"What do you mean?"

"I mean he did something in Santa Rita and picked up extra bids, ended up in San Quentin."

"What did he do?"

"I don't know."

"All right."

Belkin took a quick look at the junk that filled the room. There was a box labeled RED RUBBER BALLS — STRESS RELIEF. MEDIUM. Another box near it said COOLING SPRINGS. WARNING: KEEP DRY. It made him think about human beings and their junk. Animals in the woods didn't accumulate anything. Why did people create so much debris? Maybe that was why they killed—a deep thirst for simplicity.

The conversation was dead. He didn't want to revive it; he was too afraid that this man Rothgar would go back into the weird ranting. Then Rothgar spoke again.

"Listen, are you interested in porn? We've got some here."

"No."

"Are you sure? We've got some real outside shit. Animal stuff. Race porn. Stuff like that. You don't like it?"

"No, thanks."

"Suit yourself."

On the train home a woman mumbled to herself as she did a crossword next to Belkin. He looked at his own reflection in the tinted window across the aisle. When the train went underground his image was cast in black. Again the trauma of being shot at by Morpello came to him. Who was Morpello? Was he somehow working with the person or persons who set Pernice up? Even if that were the case, why would he want to kill Belkin? He didn't know if it was safe to go back to this house but he decided to do it anyway.

When he got home there was nobody around. His apartment wasn't too bad. The sun had already gone down but there was still some light left.

He took off his shirt and the Shield and leaned against the wall. Belkin had long avoided the Pounding but now he seemed to be thrusting his face out into the hail of blows at every opportunity. People were trying to kill him, to sell him pornography—what had happened to his routine? The Prometheus Vow was the only thing that still pegged him to the earth.

I vow to do all in my power to uncover the truth about Pernice Balfour and to restore her to the level of public decency she enjoyed before she was set up and framed by the filthy lying murderer.

The words, still memorized, resounded in his mind. He would have to clear Pernice Balfour, be done with it, and get back to staying in his room, alone, making daily computer attacks and devising rituals to muster enough energy to take out the garbage. Not that this previous life was so great, but it was better than fleeing from gunshots.

What was the next step? On the floor was a crumpled-up letter from LeCroix. Belkin remembered that this note had included LeCroix's phone number. Belkin uncrumpled the letter and called LeCroix.

"LeCroix! Have you got the photos of the evidence yet?"

"Not yet, Belky! But soon!"

"Listen. I found out that Frank Relpher went to prison. He was in prison for several years."

"Wooo! Wooo! I told you! I told you he was a very bad man, Belky!"

"Listen. Stop calling me *Belky*."

"Sorry, Royeee!"

"LeCroix! Can you get me Frank Relpher's prison record?"

"Woooo! No, I can't!"

"Too bad. I'm trying to find out as much as I can about Relpher. Somehow, he is the key."

"Woooo! Well, don't worry, Royee!"

"What is this *wooooo*? Why do you keep saying that? What's wrong with you? And why shouldn't I worry?"

"I know somebody who works in corrections, Belky. She can get anything. She's a C.O. at San Quentin."

"Well, I think he was at Santa Rita also."

"She can get *anything*, Roy. San Quentin, Santa Rita, Folsom, Pelican Bay. You name it, Cake."

"Are you sure she'll give it to you?"

"Oh yes. She's *more than just a friend*, if you know what I mean."

"Well, that would be great. LeCroix, if you could do this, it might help. I don't think Pernice Balfour committed this crime. I don't even know why I think she's the wrong one for it anymore. But I do. Anyway, LeCroix, you might not understand this, but I made a kind of a vow to clear her name. I know that it sounds strange."

"Oh, Roy! You don't have to play games with me!"

"What do you mean?"

"Well, obviously you two can't do any *praying* together if she's in jail!"

"What?"

"Well," LeCroix went on with even more insinuation in his voice, "obviously you and Sister Pernice can't *go to church* together while she is *indisposed*."

"LeCroix, I'm going to hang up the phone. I will be very grateful to you if you can see about the prison record and bring me photos of the evidence."

"Wooo!"

Belkin hung up. He was disgusted with himself for asking LeCroix for anything but there was nothing else to be done.

The next day he woke up, as always, in misery. He dragged his half-dead body out of bed. It was a Tuesday, which was one of the days Pernice Balfour was permitted to have visitors. He decided to go see her. First he drank cold coffee by the window.

An hour later, when he was face-to-face with Pernice Balfour again, they were both despondent. The guard situation around Pernice had become even more restrictive than the last time. This time there were three female correctional officers around her. One of the guards had a telescoping plastic duster, the kind used for reaching spiderwebs in ceiling corners. The guard had the soft end of the duster resting on Pernice's shoulder so that though she was at a distance she retained physical contact with her by means of the cleaning tool. Pernice didn't have the hope in her eyes that Belkin had recognized before.

"Pernice, I came here to tell you some things I found out about Frank Relpher."

"Only Lord can help me now, Mr. Belkin."

"He worked in some kind of shit-heap scrapyard out in South San Francisco. It turns out that he was a real filthy, degenerate scum, I mean even worse than I thought. But I feel that I'm closing in on a solution. I know that I lied to you, Pernice. But I feel that I'm coming closer to solving this. I actually have more hope now than before."

"Mr. Belkin, I know that you didn't mean any harm by lying. I hath forgiven you seven times seventy fold."

The guard holding the extended dust brush was absolutely impassive.

"Pernice, I'm determined to clear this thing up. I've never really committed to much as a man. To tell you the truth, I've basically always been nothing more than a reclusive motherfucking asshole . . . "

"Lord hath many mansions you know not need of," Pernice responded listlessly.

" . . . But with this, I don't know. I'm trying to make something happen here. And I know this might be hard to believe, but I'm trying to do it for you. It's like I'm trying to build a little fire out of garbage in the rain."

"Think thou therefore on the faith of thy substance. Withholdeth no hand before thy host-Lord," Pernice responded, gazing through the Plexiglas and through Belkin also.

"I mean, I'm trying. Yesterday, that detective, that ass of a detective, he ambushed me in my hallway and fired a gun at me. Can you believe it? I think he may be in on this whole thing somehow. Though I don't even really know what 'this whole thing' is."

"That which are good and true, therefore thine wine shall keep in new vessels, wherefore hith spirit guideth. Do not forsooth His sweetness."

"Well, I hope you are doing okay in here, Pernice. Try not to give up. I know this is very difficult."

"And the town people gathered themselves unto thine Lord and blesseth the host wherefore the Lord tooketh refuge when the fruit of his loins was aggrieved of him."

"Well, good-bye, Pernice."

"LORDLORD."

The visiting period ended. Belkin walked out of the building, remembering absently how public buildings used to have ashtrays with sand in them in the hallways when he was a child.

I hope I can help her, he thought.

12.

He walked from the cab to his apartment. He was still trying to get over how blank Pernice looked. He touched the Shield under his shirt, a habitual gesture. There were a few more people in the lobby of his building. He mentally bracketed them and pushed the brackets to the back of his attention, a technique he called Crushing. In his mailbox there was a check from his father's handlers in the usual blank envelope. It was always a relief when it showed up. The trouble with living on mail-money was that one had to wait for it, and no matter how often one had received it before, it always felt as if this was the time it would not arrive.

He got into the elevator and went up to his floor. He was ready to be absorbed into his apartment with its usual challenges and demands. When the elevator door opened Belkin saw that somebody was waiting outside of it. As he tried to shuffle past, he was surprised to see that the person didn't move out of the way. He looked up from the man's feet and was shocked to see that he had a brown paper bag covering his head. The bag had one hole ripped out in the area of the eyes. The figure was both frightening and ridiculous.

The man with the bag on his head punched Belkin in the face. Belkin staggered back into the elevator and hit its wall. The elevator was tiny, the size of a closet. Belkin felt more blows thudding on him as he slumped down the wall of the car. Bag-head had his foot in the door. A few more solid punches landed on Belkin's head and then Belkin was verging on unconsciousness. He felt himself being dragged down the hall on his back by the collar of his jacket. This action pulled Belkin's arms and shoulders up unnaturally into a scarecrow-like position. As he was being dragged along he noticed that the paint on the ceiling of the hall had strange brown spots. He had seen this happen before with old paint; it was called sweating. He was barely conscious. He made a connection in his mind between what was happening to him and a time when he was a boy when he had been hit in the head by a baseball. The feeling was similar. A couple of seconds later the dragging stopped and a door was pulled open. Then the dragging commenced for another few feet. Belkin was lapsing in and out of consciousness. Finally he heard the attacker speak.

"This will teach you to mind your own fucking business!"

As the words came out of the man's mouth, Belkin realized that he had been dragged into the landing of the building's stairway. He caught a glance of the man's shoes: Hush Puppies. Then the attacker lifted him up by the arms and heaved him down the steps. As he lapsed into unconsciousness, Belkin heard the man shout a final admonition from the top of the steps:

"Fuck off, asshole!"

He woke up with police, paramedics, and some neighbors around him. One of the neighbors was talking, a man in his sixties. The man had two patches of curly hair on either side of his head and somewhere in the middle there was a pair of squinting eyes under thick glasses. There were also two gray, sagging ears. Belkin knew the type: a clarinet player with bowel problems or a pill-popping TV-watching cretin.

"I found him here in a pool of blood."

Belkin was on a gurney. He was still in the landing of the stairway.

"Did you see anybody else?" a police officer asked the man.
"No."

Next, Belkin was in an ambulance. He had an IV tube stuck in his arm. What was that for? Then he slipped back into unconsciousness.

At the hospital he woke up in bandages and a horrible "gown." He saw his clothing nearby. He groaned. Soon a nurse came and then a representative of the police department, Officer Paul Morphy.

This man was black. He had skin like asphalt, a violent mustache, glasses, and a gap in his teeth. He was frighteningly muscular. *What does this guy do, pump iron all day in the squad car?* Belkin thought to himself.

"Sir, do you remember what happened?"

"I was attacked."

"By a stranger?"

"Yes. He had a bag on his head."

"A hood?"

"A bag."

"What kind of bag?"

"A paper bag."

The cop was recording everything with a handheld device. *Can you tell me the height of the attacker? Did you notice what he was wearing? Are you sure? How many times did he hit you? In the head? Anywhere else? Was his fist closed? Did he kick you?* Belkin was surprised at how specific the man got. Then the cop changed course.

"Okay, we're now going to do what is called an incident summary. I'm going to ask you to go through every detail of what happened, from the very beginning, in your own words."

Belkin recounted the whole story. He told about how he had seen the man's feet, then his head, then his fist, then the ceiling, then the stairwell, then blackness.

"Are you sure that the attacker couldn't have been anybody you know? Did you get any sense that he was targeting you personally?"

"Well, there were some people in the lobby of my building. I suppose it could have been somebody who spotted me going into the elevator and then ran up the stairs to wait for me, to wait for the elevator door to open. The bag-mask thing seemed pretty improvised. If that were the case, the person would have to know me well enough to know what floor I was going to get off on."

"Can you think of anybody who might have that kind of information?"

"No."

After a few more questions the cop left. Belkin stayed at the hospital. He was still plugged into an IV. He had a neighbor in the room, an old man who mumbled in Spanish. After a while he was wheeled into another room, where they put staples in his skull. That night he slept densely but was awakened by a nurse over and over again to make sure he hadn't lapsed into a coma. The nurse told him he had a concussion.

The next morning a doctor checked his skull and then they released him. He hadn't told the police officer that the attacker had told him to "mind his own fucking business." To do so would initiate a whole separate conversation that he didn't want to get into. At this point he wasn't sure if the police could be trusted. If the half-wit Morpello really had it in for him, he might somehow use this incident to get close and strike. Belkin decided that he would work it out with his only known ally, Emile LeCroix.

"Pathetic," Belkin said as he painstakingly limped through the lobby of his building. The morning was starchy and full of aches. Coffee meant nothing to him. He was on pills.

That whole day he was at home, bedridden. Pain was every-where. Druggy sleep came and went. He had a bruised rib and his jaw was elongated. He had lost a tooth and his body was discol-ored—green, black, blue, yellow, and orange. He felt like a soft, rotten fruit. Already weak before the stairway thrashing, now he was like human compost.

In his sleep he dreamed of the man with the bag on his head. In one feverish interval, Belkin dreamed that the hallway attacker was driving nails into his skull. Then a knock came. It took a long time to get over to the front door and the effort wasn't exactly rewarded—it was LeCroix. Any time there was a knock or a phone call he had an irrational hope that it would be Pernice.

LeCroix was with a fat woman wearing a tan pantsuit. LeCroix had a gray velour jumpsuit on and silver sneakers. He was sweating and grinning peevishly. The woman was taller than both LeCroix and Belkin and had short hair that was cut in the style of a man Belkin had seen on television once, an Australian who liked to play with snakes. The woman was standing behind LeCroix and leering at Belkin.

"Roy! I heard what happened! This is Babbith Marisol. She's my friend from San Quentin! She wanted to come by personally to give you the information that you asked about, brother!"

Belkin retreated back to his bed. Babbith and LeCroix followed him and hovered over him like a pair of undertakers. Finally Babbith spoke.

"You're right Emile, he's a real sweet piece of pie."

"God yes, Babbith."

"He's hot stuff."

Belkin groaned and rolled away from them until his face was against the wall.

"You should see him dance!" LeCroix said.

The two of them were speaking with indulgent tones as if trying to cheer Belkin up with flattery.

"I would *love* to see him dance."

"He's the emperor's miracle!" LeCroix went on.

"*Niiiice.*"

"You have no idea *how* nice, lady-cop. Anyway, Roy, I know you only care about one thing, so maybe these will make you feel better."

LeCroix dropped an envelope on the bed. Belkin rolled over and took it.

"Mr. Belkin, I know you are out of sorts, but Emile said you wanted to hear about Frank Relpher," the woman said.

In his battered state Belkin had forgotten that LeCroix had told him about a friend who worked in corrections. It came to him. This was the woman, the woman with the information. She sat down in the chair he normally sat in.

"Yes . . . you knew him?" Belkin said, perking up a bit.

"No, but I was able to look at his record."

"What did it say?"

"Well, he originally got a six-month sentence at Santa Rita, which is for short-timers. But then he got charged with having a weapon in the jail a couple times. So he ended up being sent to San Quentin for one year. Then he got a series of violations. I talked to somebody from San Quentin who was in charge of tossing cells for contraband. My friend remembered Relpher. He told me that Relpher was a guy who made weapons, stoves, tattoo guns, and other mechanical stuff for other prisoners. Kind of a prison mechanic."

"Really? What else did he tell you?" Belkin was leaning forward and sitting up.

"Well, here, I took some notes. I couldn't make a copy of the records but for a friend of Emile"—Babbith looked at her sweating companion with her eyebrows raised and her mouth open—"I'll go to great lengths. You see, I shouldn't even really be telling you *anything*. Anyway," Babbith went on, now reading from a slip of paper she had taken out of her pocket, "over the course of a year they caught Relpher with two knives, materials that could be used to make a zip gun, and a grenade."

"A grenade?"

"Yes, a kind of prison grenade. It's made with a yogurt container, rubber bands, ground-up light bulbs, and cleaning agents."

"What was the other thing you said he had?"

"A zip gun?"

"Yeah, what's that?" Belkin asked.

"It's an implement that can fire a bullet like a gun. It can also fire other projectiles, depending on the design. They either get a real bullet somehow or grind up match heads and lighter flints to shoot something else. It's basically a homemade firearm."

"Hmm," Belkin said.

"Well, that's all I really have, Mr. Belkin. Frank Relpher ended up doing four years, all because of contraband and stuff in his cells. After a while he cleaned up his act and just did his time, or else he managed to stop getting caught."

"I see. Well, thank you, that's very helpful," Belkin said from the mattress. Perking back up had made him conscious of the bandages and the pain again.

Babbith Marisol looked at Belkin. Emile LeCroix was standing next to her grinning and shifting his weight from one foot to the other.

"Amazing, isn't he?" LeCroix said.

"Mmm," Babbith responded. "I know he's in bad shape right now but *wow*. *Yes*, Emile. *Nice*."

"Haha! Oh, Babbith! That's what I love about you! You know a good piece of meat when you see it!"

"Oh yeah, Emile. It's like, *Hello*! Right? It's like, *Oh yeah!* I mean, I'd like to learn about his *foam*."

"Oh, God!" responded LeCroix. "It's like, *Yeah! Yeah!*"

"I don't know how you do it, Emile, but you always find them. I wonder if it's that little picture machine you hang around your neck? I wish I could reel them in like you do," Babbith said.

"Oh, Babbith! You got *me*, didn't you?" As he said it he straddled her leg playfully.

"Wheee!" she shouted.

Belkin wanted to throw up. "LeCroix, where did you find somebody . . . like *you*?"

"Haha! You're right, Belko! She's a kindred soul. You're not going to believe it but I met her in church!"

"It's hard to believe," Belkin said.

He didn't believe or not believe. He was ready for the two of them to get out.

"Well, I hope that was helpful, Mr. Belkin," said Babbith. "Maybe when you feel better you would like to do a scene with me and Emile?"

"I don't think so."

"Okay," said LeCroix, "We'll see you tomorrow."

"No! No!" Belkin shouted as they left and closed the door behind them.

They were gone. He opened the envelope LeCroix had given him. There were several photos. There was a note.

Dear Roy,

Can't wait to see ya! Here are the photos. I wrote some descriptive information on each one based on the forensic reports. Yawn. I guess by the time you see this note, I actually will have seen you and you will have seen me—and Babbith. I am looking forward to that. I was hoping the three of us could get together in a private setting, if you know what I mean—perhaps in March if you feel up for it.

Sin-cerely,

Emile LeCroix

Belkin glanced at the photos. Affixed to each one by a paper clip was a three-by-five card on which LeCroix had written notes. In spite of the unclean feeling that Belkin always experienced after LeCroix left, and in spite of his pain, he was grateful for the information. He had been loping and stumbling along and he wanted to be justified in some way. He looked at the photos one after another and read the notes.

The first photo was a handgun. The handgun looked strange and antique. It was in a plastic evidence bag.

This is the murder weapon found in Pernice Balfour's apartment. It is a unique handgun that was made in the sixties called a Pisces Fox which fires a shotgun shell rather than a normal bullet.

The second photo was of a jar containing an amber-colored fluid. Like the gun, it was in an evidence bag. Affixed to the outside of the bag were warning labels that said HIGHLY COMBUSTIBLE.

This jar contains high-density cleaning solvents, motor oil, and industrial glues. It is very flammable and is the same as traces of the chemical cocktail found in Relpher's apartment at the point of origin of the fire. This was found in Pernice Balfour's apartment along with the gun. The police suspect it is an accelerant (fire-starting mixture).

The next photo was of a bunch of debris, much like the stuff that Belkin had seen all around Relpher's apartment. It was a pile of burned garbage that included pipes, pieces of wood, coat hangers, and broken coffee mugs. It was all arranged in plastic bags on a white table.

This is the debris found in close proximity to Frank Relpher's body. Wow—isn't this fun? I'm KIDDING! By the way, L.A. was a blast! Did you know that you can freebase cocaine through other parts of the body than just the mouth? IF YOU KNOW WHAT I MEAN.

The next photo was of a letter in an evidence bag. Belkin read LeCroix's description of the item:

Yawn. Here's the letter.

Then Belkin read the letter itself. The letter was typed on an old-fashioned typewriter and was enlarged in the photograph enough that one could make out the words.

ATTENTION SAN FRANCISCO HOMICIDE DEPARTMENT
The arsonist is pernice balfour. She lives in
the same pierce street building that was just
burned in apt. 211. You can find the murder
weapon and other items in her bedroom closet.
I am close to this and i know what's going
on. Here is the proof: i know that relpher
was killed with a shotgun shell and that you
found photos of pernice balfour in relpher's
apartment.

The next photo was of what looked like a charred matchbook.
It was in a plastic bag like the other stuff.

*This is an incendiary device. The forensics team examined
it. The matchbook had a lit cigarette tucked into the matches
with the burning end out and away from them. The whole
thing is bound up or taped. When the cigarette burns down,
the matches ignite. This was found at the origin point of the
fire in Relpher's apartment.*

There was one more photograph. This one was of a small,
cylindrical metal cap. It was in a bag like the other items and it
was charred black. Unlike the other photographs, that had notes
LeCroix wrote on three-by-five cards, this one had a full letter,
like the kind LeCroix had been slipping under Belkin's door.

*Dear Roy,
   This is a shell casing. Forensics confirmed that it was fired*

from the murder weapon—the antique gun they found in Pernice's apartment. This was found near the body at the crime scene.

God this is boring Roy. I think you need a hobby. Have you tried yoga? I have—it's terrible! LOL! Don't do it Roy! At least not at that studio down on Van Ness Street. It's full of old men. The yoga teacher knows it and she's always coming up with poses where you're staring right up into their assholes. I don't know why she doesn't just say it: "Okay class, everybody find an old man and plant your face in his fat, sagging ass!" What a goddamned bitch. Anyway, like I said, DON'T DO IT. But if you do, take some pictures! LOL! By the way, all this information that I got for you I got by reading the forensics report. THAT I can't photograph for you—it would be going too far. Sorry, "Pappy."

With Vigour,

Emile LeCroix

P.S. Stay RAW, Roy. the world wants to slow people like you and me down.

After reading the letters and looking at the photos, Roy lay in bed. There were hours of pain and bad sleep. He thought about the evidence. Then he would fall asleep for an hour. It went on like this. Next he would wake up aching again. His ribs hurt as well as his arm and head. The doctor at the hospital said there was "some swelling of the brain."

He was restless. He was too depressed and injured to perform his usual computer activities. He lay there thinking about the case. After several hours of swollen, aching thought he got up and looked up "prison weapons" on the computer. The pages came shuffling into his consciousness. He read about shanks, clubs, prison sling-shots, poison darts made from ballpoint pens, socks and locks (self-explanatory), and zip guns. It was fascinating. The resourcefulness of these convicts was impressive. One prisoner made a shank out of hardened chewing gum and bread dough, which he successfully stabbed somebody with. Every prison had a confiscated cache of weapons that had been created out of plastic, wood, metal, and glass. In the section on zip guns there was only one page of pho-tographs of confiscated devices. Some fired an actual bullet; others fired homemade projectiles. There was a story about a man who had made a zip gun out of a shower pipe and had somehow gotten hold of a bullet. He and a partner were going to try to escape with it, but when he fired the weapon the bullet went in the wrong direc-tion and blinded his accomplice. Finally Belkin looked at a section on "gassing," or saving up human waste to throw in the faces of correctional officers. The last bit was all he could take.

He got back in bed with one of his yellow legal pads, deter-mined to get back to work in spite of the pain. *I've got to get organized*, he thought. He tried to write down what he knew in some kind of logical sequence:

1. THERE WAS A STRING OF ARSONS
2. ONE HAPPENED IN MY BUILDING AND FRANK RELPHER WAS KILLED IN IT
3. I SUSPECT THAT FRANK RELPHER WAS THE ARSONIST? (MAYBE)
4. MAYBE HE HAD A PARTNER WHO KILLED HIM
5. ANYWAY, THE KILLER THEN FRAMED PERNICE

(AFTER KILLING RELPHER)

6. THE KILLER WOULD HAVE TO BE CLOSE TO FRANK RELPHER TO KNOW ABOUT HIS RELATIONSHIP WITH PERNICE AND CHOOSE HER FOR THE FRAME UP

7. EVEN IF I AM WRONG AND PERNICE ACTUALLY DID KILL RELPHER THAT STILL LEAVES THE QUESTION OF WHO TIPPED OFF THE POLICE ABOUT THE STUFF IN HER APARTMENT (BUT I'M NOT WRONG—SHE DIDN'T DO IT).

8. I DON'T KNOW WHAT HAPPENED

9. WHAT'S THE POINT OF LIVING ANYWAY? THE WORLD IS SHIT . . . SHIT

He could tell the list was degenerating, so he put down the pad. Then he picked it up again. He read the facts. They didn't make any sense. He wrote down a summary:

CONCLUSION: THE ONLY LOGICAL THING I CAN COME UP WITH IS THAT FRANK RELPHER AND THE KILLER WERE SOMEHOW BOTH INVOLVED WITH THE ARSONS. MAYBE RELPHER HELPED THE KILLER OR MAYBE RELPHER WAS THE ARSONIST AND THE KILLER KNEW HIM VERY WELL AND WAS AWARE OF HIS M.O. THE PERSON WHO COMMITTED THIS ARSON/MURDER THEN FRAMED PERNICE BALFOUR, PRESUMABLY TO DETER SUSPICION FROM HIMSELF.

After writing it down he found that he was exhausted. He went to sleep.

The next day Roy went to visit his father. His face in the mirror looked bad. He decided to go because he thought that the sight of his condition might shock his father into some kind of response. When he got there, however, he saw only Hoose. Hoose was doing something with a computer that was inside an open briefcase on the kitchen table. Ms. Calbenza was out shopping.

"Your father is on extended sleep."

Belkin knew what it meant. His father would occasionally sleep for three or four days straight. It seemed to be some kind of self-repairing hibernation process that compensated for his high brain activity. Belkin never tried to bother him during those periods. Instead he sat at the kitchen table with Hoose.

"Agent Hoose, aren't you going to comment on my face?"

"Roy, I'm not an agent. Secondly, we already know about the incident and the personal damage you accrued so there's no point feigning a reaction."

"You already know about it?"

"I didn't say that."

"Yes, you did."

The room fell silent. Hoose was behind the dark glasses. Belkin drank coffee that Ms. Calbenza had prepared before she left.

"Well, do you know who did it, for God's sake? I could have been killed. Which is something that I am indifferent to but you shouldn't be. I mean, I don't think you should be. Should you? Be indifferent?"

"Actually, I should be, but I'm not. You can trust that we are taking the appropriate measures. Don't trust that we are doing anything or know who it was who attacked you, but trust *in the act of trusting us*. You can be totally certain that is the right course of action."

"Okay, Hoose."

Again with the silence. This guy is worse than Father Basil, Roy thought. Then something occurred to him, a question he had been meaning to ask Agent Hoose for some time.

"Listen, Hoose, you've dealt with my father for years. Probably more than any human being should really, aside from

Ms. Calbenza. And I mean, she has her own problems. Anyway, what do you think is wrong with him? Do you have any idea?"

"As far as our needs our concerned, there is nothing wrong with him."

"What are your needs?"

"I can't tell you that."

"What does he do exactly?"

Belkin had asked the question before but was never satisfied with the answer. He imagined he would ask it every so often for the rest of his life.

"We receive information that is so encrypted that it lacks all meaning. We rely on your father to decrypt it. Conversely, we need to encode things with such obscurity that the enemy will never be able to decipher them. Your father helps with that also."

"Why does the code have to be so dense?"

"The enemy has an operative similar to your father, a code savant."

"Really? Like my father? Who is?"

"We only know that he is called the Raja."

"You're kidding. Did you make that up?"

"You shouldn't even know about it."

"Why are you telling me?"

"It's part of our job to reveal a certain percentage of classified information. It's been found that it prevents larger leaks if there is a constant but small stream of disclosure going on."

"Well, don't worry about me, Hoose. I'm with you guys, 100 percent."

"I'll be the judge of that."

"Well, who is 'the enemy' anyway?"

"This conversation just ceased to exist."

"Why, because I asked who the enemy is? Isn't that the CIA's job? To spread fear about the enemy? To gather fear-data?"

"I'm going to have to ask you to eat that question."

"Consider it done."

"The CIA is to us what a toy airplane would be to a fleet of UFOs. We never work with solids, only with abstractions. Gaseous intelligence. Even so, things need to be encrypted. If I am contacting an operative in Japan and I need to let him know that his current overview is skewed, I have to avoid allowing my message to fall into the realm of enemy consumption. When we convey information, often the recipient doesn't even know that he's received it. We deal with clouds of data, not factoids. Your father is like a weatherman."

"Wow."

"That's all I'm going to say about it."

"All right."

They sat there for a while. Hoose clacked away at the keyboard inside his briefcase and Belkin drank the coffee. It was relatively peaceful. In spite of his anxiety about his father, Belkin always felt comfortable at his father's apartment. Maybe it was because between Ulmers, Hoose, and Calbenza there was always something getting done. The constant activity allowed Roy not to drive himself. It was a respite from all the petty guilt he experienced in his own house.

"Well, Mr. Hoose, I'm going to leave now."

"We paid your hospital deductible."

"Thanks."

Behind the dark glasses and the gaseous intelligence, Hoose's head nodded one quarter of an inch.

14.

Belkin went home. The pain came back, particularly around one of his shoulders. He took pills and slept. He was awakened at eleven that night by a knock on the door. He went to the door. There was a police officer there.

"Yes?"

"Are you Roy Belkin?"

"Yes."

"I'm here because we apprehended a suspect in your assault

complaint. We want you to come down to the police station and identify him."

"Isn't it a bit late at night for that?"

"The homicide detective has connected this assault to the murder that took place here three weeks ago. He wants to talk to you."

"Bud Morpello?"

"Yes, Detective Bud Morpello."

"I won't go."

"Sir, if you refuse to come down, I am going to have to arrest you."

"What? For what?"

"I'm sorry, sir. I know that it is unconventional, but Detective Morpello is the best goddamned detective in this city and is given a wider latitude than most officers. He instructed me to arrest you if you didn't come down voluntarily."

Belkin put on his shoes. Part of the reason he was submitting, aside from the fact that resistance seemed to be pointless, was that he had just about lost the will to live. If Morpello used this incident to kill him somehow, at least he would die in the process of trying to fulfill the Prometheus Vow. It would be for a cause. The death would be kind of a free pass—an easy exit without the moral ambiguity of suicide.

During the car ride to the police station, Belkin was in a mental and physical stupor. He couldn't do anything else as far as this case went. He had gotten nowhere, really. Nothing of significance had been determined. He was no closer to exonerating Pernice Balfour than he had been the day he had met her. And now it seemed that he was being delivered right into the hands of somebody who wanted to kill him. It no longer mattered why. It was clearly time to give up. Not just on the case but also on life, the hope of reason, sanity, everything. He felt himself fading in the backseat of the police car. A dark revelation took place in his psyche: that this moment was the very low point of his life.

The officer led him past desk clerks and other administrative types. His life was in danger but everybody was just typing away at their little keyboards. The banality of it all seemed to parallel the plight of the world at large. The apocalypse was no longer being driven by the roar of factories; it was now being driven by the *clickety-clack* of keyboards. The cop walked next to him as they went to the back of the station, to Bud Morpello's office. Belkin was led through the door.

Bud Morpello was behind his desk with his mouth open and eyes half-closed. Once again the room was very dark, but Belkin could make out that there were two men seated near Morpello. One of the men looked like another detective. The other one was in handcuffs. He looked familiar to Belkin. He had dark curly hair, unruly eyebrows, and angry moles on his face.

Belkin stood in front of Morpello's desk.

"Mr. Belking?" Morpello asked.

"Yes."

"This is Police Commissioner Louis Peyton."

The man seated next to Morpello nodded. This boded well, Belkin thought. Morpello probably wouldn't try to kill him with the commissioner there.

"Oh."

"This other man is the man who beat you up, Kevin Deasly."

Belkin looked at the man in handcuffs, who glowered back at

him. He looked to be about the same size. It was plausible that it was the same guy.

"How do you know?" Belkin asked.

"One of your neighbors came forward."

"Who is he?" Belkin said.

"I'm your neighbor in apartment 218, asshole!" the man shouted from his seat.

"What? Why did you attack me?"

"Because you keep leaving fucking notes on my door!"

"What? Oh my God! You're the one with the diaper service?"

The man rolled his eyes.

"He attacked me because I left notes on his door when he left bags of human-infant-waste in the hall!" Belkin shouted.

"Is this true?" Morpello asked the man in handcuffs.

"Yes," the man said.

There was silence and a long pause.

Here we go, Belkin thought. The man that Morpello had referred to as a police commissioner said nothing.

Finally, Morpello spoke. "Say you're sorry."

Kevin Deasly glanced back and forth between Belkin and Morpello. "I'm sorry," he said.

"Okay, Larry, let him go," Morpello said to the cop who had escorted Belkin in.

"What? Let him go? He tried to kill me! This is a psychopath you're dealing with! Are you out of your mind?"

The cop took the man's handcuffs off. Morpello continued to sit without moving. Belkin's attacker rushed out the door of the office before Morpello could change his mind.

"I can't believe this!" Belkin shouted. "You brought me down here so you could let this guy go? Listen, Commissioner," Belkin implored the other man, "this Morpello—something is wrong with him! You may not believe what I am about to tell you, but this man came to my apartment building and fired his gun at me! I was just walking down my hall and there he was blasting away! You can still see the bullet holes in the wall!"

The commissioner looked at Belkin and then at Bud Morpello.

"Detective Morpello, is this true?"

"I think so," Morpello answered.

"Why did you shoot at him?"

"I thought he was a suspect."

"I see." The commissioner looked back at Belkin as if Morpello had just explained everything.

"What? That's good enough for you? 'I thought he was a suspect'? What does that mean? Who is this guy? What's wrong with you people?"

"Mr. Belkin, you may think that Detective Morpello's methods are unusual, but it just so happens that he is one of the best god-damned cops this city has ever seen. So if he says he had a good reason, that's good enough for me."

Belkin felt dizzy. He slumped down into the chair that his attacker had been sitting in. Morpello spoke next.

"Larry, arrest Mr. Belking."

"Yes, sir."

The police officer who had escorted him in took Belkin's arm and guided him up and into a pair of handcuffs.

"Arrest me? What are you arresting *me* for?"

The room was silent. The question hung in the air. Morpello and the commissioner sat there. The police officer stood next to

Belkin. Though it was dark, Belkin could make out that the commissioner was looking at Morpello inquisitively. Finally Morpello
spoke.

"Resisting arrest."

"Ahhh," the commissioner said.

Belkin simply stopped talking. The police officer led him out
of Morpello's office and back down the hall and then across a
breezeway into a building next door that held the jail. He was
processed there. Belkin did not try to reason with anybody. It was
clear that the justice system was a world of madmen, apparently
ruled by the idiot-king Bud Morpello.

After the paperwork he was taken to a cell. He expected to
hear shouting and jeering and see prisoners playing cards and
spitting on the floor. Instead he ended up in what seemed to be a
remote part of the building. The cell was large and at the end of
a long hall. There was another man in it. Belkin stepped into the
room and the cop took off his handcuffs. As the police officer was
closing the door Belkin asked him, "What is this cell? Why aren't
there other people around?"

"Oh, this is called the expected recognizance cell. It's for prisoners that we expect to release within twelve hours. It's mainly
used for the homeless and chronic alcoholics who come through
here over and over again."

"Why are you putting me in here?"

"When Detective Morpello has somebody arrested, he usually
forgets about them and we end up letting them go after a few
hours."

"Why don't you just let me go now?"

"Procedure."

The door closed.

The room was fairly large and dark, clearly some kind of holding tank. The walls were gray. There was a man sitting in one corner. Belkin sat as far away from the man as possible. The misery he was experiencing had reached such a depth that he no longer cared about anything. It was a new nadir, a few steps lower than what he had experienced earlier in the police car. Suicide was out of the question—too embarrassing. But barring that he thought he would still find some way to die through sheer apathy within a month or so. He realized that he was drifting off to sleep. He was still aching from the stairway beating.

The man sitting across the cell from him got up and walked over. Belkin saw him and wished he could think of some way to discourage him. He was a disheveled, bearded vagrant of some kind. He had red hair and the sunburn of somebody who took afternoon naps on the sidewalk. He looked like a motorcycle gang member but much more haggard—a wino.

"Red," he said as he stood in front of Belkin. Now that he was close Belkin could see that he was about five and a half feet tall and in his fifties.

"What?"

"The name's Red."

"Oh. I'm Roy Belkin."

The man sat down next to Roy on the bench. Belkin tensed up. This could be some kind of jail assault waiting to happen. He realized that it was important to "respect" Red but to do so without "backing down." But when Red spoke again it was in a friendly, paternal tone.

"I suppose you don't spend much time in jail."

"No, this is actually my first time."

"Ha! How'd I guess? Let's see—Bud Morpello have you arrested?"

"Yes! Yes! How did you know that?"

"Well, I end up here pretty often because I get a little loose when I have too much to drink. Half the time I show up, there is some poor fool here that jackass Morpello has sent through the ringer."

"Wow!" Belkin exclaimed. "I mean, to finally talk to some-body who understands that there is something wrong with that man . . . "

"Something wrong with him? He's a complete fucking idiot!"

"Ha! You got that right, Mister! I thought the whole world was going crazy!" Belkin replied.

"Well, don't worry about it, man. You should be out of here within a day or two."

Belkin's internal organs sank into themselves. "Within a day or two? But that cop just told me . . . "

"Aww shit, brother. Sorry to be the one to tell you. They just say that to people to keep them calm. Anyway, most I've ever seen one of Morpello's 'suspects' in here for was a week or two. I wouldn't worry about it."

Belkin felt sick. He couldn't stop himself from lying down on the bench. There were some cots in the cell but he was too tired to even make it over to them. The fatigue that came over him didn't feel personal. It was the fatigue of an age, of a city, maybe the fatigue of the whole history of the human enterprise with its billions of dis-appointed people plodding through the muck toward the open pit of death. As he began to drift off to sleep Red kept talking to him.

"Don't worry, man. Believe it or not, I know how it is the first time you get put in jail. Kind of makes a person redefine themselves. I mean, no matter how tough you are, once you get in here it's the first time you know you can be turned into a *thing*. You know what I mean? Shit, I been in here so many times I'm over the shock of it."

Belkin listened to Red's voice. It was soothing. He felt safe around the guy though he had just met him. After a while Belkin drifted off to sleep. The man was still talking. He lapsed into a dream in which he was a hobo in a train car with Red, listening as the older man told him stories from a life on the rails.

Hours later he woke up. He saw that across the cell a couple more shabby, bearded men had shown up. They were all talking loudly. When he moved, Red walked across the cell to him.

"Look, Roy, I know you're probably a little unused to these surroundings. Just to let you know, don't worry about anything. All these guys know me and I'm kind of like a leader around here. Not that there's any problem anyway. All these guys are basically harmless. Just bums, you know. I mean, don't worry. Sleep it off, brother."

Too tired to think about it, Belkin shut his eyes again. As he did he listened to the conversations going on in the cell. He heard Red talking to the others:

"Listen here, assholes, quiet it down a little bit. Nobody is saying you can't talk but if you're all screaming it makes me feel fuckin' crazy."

"Red, I was just . . . "

"What did I say to you? Shut the fuck up! And see that guy over there? Nobody fuck with him! Understand?"

Then the conversation lapsed into the background as Belkin slipped into the lower depths of his mind. Here, all the elements of the Frank Relpher murder swam around one another. He saw Pernice Balfour holding a Bible and moving her lips soundlessly. He saw Relpher's apartment, the pornographic photos, the basement, Father Basil, Rothgar's Salvage, and the photo of Frank Relpher being surprised in the bathroom. He found himself in the bathtub reciting the Prometheus Vow over and over again. He saw Morpello slowly raising his arm and firing a gun at him. He imagined Frank Relpher as a prison inmate fashioning weapons and smuggling them out into the yard. Then he disappeared into complete unconsciousness.

In his next sentient moment, Belkin was dreaming. He was in the desert. In the dream, he knew the place to be ancient Israel. There was a very short, stocky, dark, and ugly man standing before him. He knew the man to be Jesus. *Oh, so this is what the real Jesus looked like*, he thought. *I should ask him something before I wake up.* Though the man was standing right in front of him, Belkin felt as though he had to shout in the dream as though across a busy street.

"Jesus! Jesus! Tell me! WHO KILLED FRANK RELPHER!"

The Jesus of his dream showed no indication of having heard the question. Still, he started mumbling back to Belkin in an ancient language that was full of guttural sounds.

"*Machlam bacholog gugh luph flamakbar machgh glab . . .* "

"WHAT? WHAT? I CAN'T UNDERSTAND YOU!"

"*Acham laphagah buloghma ba la fa ma bagh.*"

Jesus was staring at Roy but really into the distance behind him, as if through a hole in Roy's chest. His tone was not that of a person imparting wisdom but instead the matter-of-fact banter of somebody giving directions or talking about the weather. A cow walked by in the background just behind Jesus. It turned and glanced at Belkin and then kept loping along. Belkin could make out that something was written in mud on the side of the cow. "FUCK YOU," it read. Jesus continued to mumble unintelligibly.

Ha! This guy is just as useless in a dream as he is in real life! Belkin thought.

Then he was at home in the shower. The warm water ran down his face. It seemed to wash away all the pain, all the squalor and debasement of the last two weeks. He was still partially aware that he was dreaming and very quickly this turned into a greater and greater sense of waking up. The dreaded remembrance that he was in a jail came to him slowly, heavily. The dream sensation of water splashing on his face continued. Then he realized it:

Somebody was urinating on his face.

He opened his eyes into tiny slits. Through them, with the urine still landing on him, he could make out hazy figures.

Red was standing over him and there were three other men in a single-file line. The first man in the line was the one who was relieving himself.

"Awww yeah, man . . . that's good . . . awwww . . . " he said as he did it. "That's real nice, Red."

"Quiet! You're going to wake him up!" Red answered. "Three cigarettes," Red said to the next man in line, who quickly replaced the first one.

The next man in line handed Red the cigarettes and began unzipping his pants.

"I'm gonna piss on him real good, Red! This is gonna be real sweet!"

Like Red, all three of the men were shabby transients, obviously winos. Belkin didn't care. As far as he was concerned, they could set him on fire. It was over. Everything was over. The third man in the group spoke. He was fatter than the others and wore an ancient T-shirt that said "DISCO SUCKS."

"Hey, Red—I'll blow you if you let me shit on him!"

Belkin stirred but not out of any effort to prevent the goings-on. Red noticed the slight movement.

"All right, you assholes! Act fuckin' normal! He's waking up!"

The three men shambled back to different areas of the holding pen. Red hovered over Belkin.

"Hey, buddy—you okay? You was kinda mumbling in your sleep. That's why I came over here."

Belkin said something that Red couldn't hear clearly.

"What's that? Huh?" Red asked.

Belkin sat up and opened his eyes.

"I know who killed Frank Relpher," he said.

15.

A couple of hours later, the guard came to release Belkin. Red had lied about Morpello's suspects being detained for days on end. Presumably he just wanted to lure Belkin to go to sleep so he could charge his friends to urinate on him, Belkin thought. He had been allowed to take a shower when he told the jail captain that the transients had pissed on him.

"They'll do that," the captain said.

Now Belkin sat in a chair facing Detective Morpello's desk.

When Belkin had asked if he could see them again he was whisked right back up to Morpello's office. Morpello was in there as well as the commissioner and the cop who had originally showed up at his apartment. Apparently the commissioner had been in there for six hours, since he was sitting in the exact same place as when Belkin had been arrested. Belkin wasn't surprised by anything anymore. These men seemed to move and think like ghosts.

"Detective Morpello, Commissioner Peyton, I have thought for a long time about this case."

"I'm glad you thought about it. I can't figure it out," Morpello said.

"Let's hear it, man," Peyton agreed.

"Well, I've been running around, talking to people, talking to Pernice Balfour and so on and so forth, and one thing has bothered me throughout. Frank Relpher was a bit of a recluse, a strange guy who I happen to know was also a burglar and possibly a sociopath, right?"

"Who is Frank Relpher?" Morpello asked.

"He is the one who was killed."

"Oh."

"Furthermore, I did a little research on him and I found out that he was in prison for four years. Now while he was in prison, he was a sort of *prison mechanic*. He built things for people. Weapons, contraband, and so on. He got in trouble for this and eventually cut it out, but the point is he knew how to make that stuff."

"How did you find out he was in prison?" Morpello asked.

"I asked somebody about him."

"Oh."

"Anyway, the thing bothering me was this: the coincidence of this mysterious arsonist breaking into Frank Relpher's apartment. I mean, there is something odd about one antisocial criminal breaking into another antisocial criminal's apartment."

"I didn't think of that," Morpello answered.

Commissioner Peyton looked on.

"Well, my initial solution was this: Frank Relpher was somehow involved with the arsonist. In other words, he was a partner to him or something. But that still didn't help. I mean, that didn't get Pernice Balfour off the hook. You see, I've been convinced that somebody killed Frank Relpher and set up Pernice Balfour."

"The Bible lady?" Morpello asked.

"Yes."

"She didn't kill him?"

"No."

"Why didn't you tell us?"

"I did. I tried to. You didn't listen to me."

"Yes, I did," Morpello answered.

"I've been going over it in my mind and coming up with nothing. Actually the answer is so obvious that I completely overlooked it. And here it is: there *was* only one arsonist. That arsonist killed Frank Relpher and that arsonist set up Pernice Balfour."

"Who was it?" Commissioner Peyton asked.

"It was Frank Relpher."

"Who?" Morpello said.

"Let me run it down for you from the beginning. Frank Relpher was an unhappy person who went around San Francisco setting people's apartment buildings on fire in his spare time. The reason he found it so easy to do this was that he had all the skills and equipment necessary to break into people's apartments while they weren't there. Once inside he would set up a timed incendiary device at his leisure.

"One day, he met a woman in his own apartment building. This woman, Pernice Balfour, gave him hope. She happened to have a kind of innocent beauty that makes some men think there is still good in the world. To make matters worse, she agreed to go out with him a couple of times. I'm sure Relpher was stunned at his good luck. When she broke it off, Relpher became very discouraged and angry. He even threatened the woman, saying 'I am going to ruin your life.' By that time he had come up with a plan.

"The next thing he did was break into her apartment and steal some photographs. At the same time he put a box deep in her closet where she wouldn't find it. The box contained a unique handgun and some fire-starting chemicals, the same kind he had used in the arsons. By the way, before he planted the handgun he made sure to fire it so that it would show signs of having been discharged recently.

"Around the time of this burglary he wrote a note to the police department providing an anonymous tip accusing Pernice Balfour of the arson/murder. When the police got it, they believed it because it had details about the crime that only an insider could know. It never occurred to them that the note had been sent *before* the crime had been committed. Relpher died on a Sunday afternoon. He probably dropped the letter in a mailbox on a Saturday night, which means it wouldn't be postmarked until Monday, the day *after* he was killed."

"Well, how did he shoot himself with a gun he had already planted in Miss Balfour's house?" Commisioner Peyton asked.

"That's the part I didn't figure out until about an hour ago. Frank Relpher, the prison contraband engineer, built a device that would fire a shotgun shell into his skull but be unrecognizable once it was consumed by a fire. The reason he planted a handgun that fired a shotgun shell in Pernice's apartment, as opposed to a regular handgun that fires a bullet, is that you can't match a shotgun round to the gun that fired it. In other words, forensics would never be able to figure out that the bullet that killed Relpher had not actually been fired from the weapon found in Pernice Balfour's apartment, only that the gun had been fired recently. On that Sunday, he put a pile of junk together on the floor, which wasn't hard to do because his apartment was full of clutter. Next he dumped chemicals all over it, propped himself on top of the whole mess in a chair, set up the homemade gun, and blew his brains out. He had set a timed incendiary device to start the fire after he was dead—a cigarette tucked into a book of matches. The material was already planted in Pernice's apartment and the note was already in the mailbox."

"Wait a second, Mr. Belkin," Commissioner Peyton said. "We found a shell case at the scene of the crime. It was five feet away from the body and undamaged. That makes it consistent with having been fired by an assailant."

"It was a prop. Relpher had to discharge the gun before he planted it to make it fit as a murder weapon. After he fired the handgun he kept the shell and left it on the floor near where he was going to stage the murder. The *real* shell is still lodged inside the apparatus that he used to kill himself.

"The device had to be some variation of a zip gun, a home-made weapon usually designed to fire a single bullet. I saw some versions of this thing when I was looking at prison weapons on the computer. I imagine in the evidence you will find a metal pipe that at some point had a cap on the end and a small hole drilled in the back of the cap. The shell was inserted at the open end and pushed down to where the pipe was capped off. The firing pin is usually a nail that goes through the back powered by a rubber band or a balloon or anything really. You can use a mousetrap spring or an electrical charge from a battery. After he was dead, the fire he set up consumed the whole thing. I imagine he made as much of the device as possible out of highly flammable parts. Two or three days later, the letter arrived at the police department. Pernice Balfour was picked up and Frank Relpher fulfilled his promise to 'ruin her life.' He was probably looking for a way out anyway. This gave his suicide a purpose.

"Frank Relpher was a miserable person who was full of hate and a sense of impotency. I could tell by the look on his face in a photograph and by his apartment vibrations. When Pernice Balfour rejected him, it made no difference why or whether or not she had a good reason. He started scheming. He used his background knowledge to come up with the plan to make it look like she killed him. Not only that but that she was an arsonist. The anonymous note was the final touch. But I never believed that Pernice Balfour was capable of it. And so that's what happened. Frank Relpher killed *himself*."

The room was silent. Bud Morpello sat absolutely still, as if he were a carefully constructed man-shell that had been filled with wet clay. Commissioner Louis Peyton sat next to him. The police officer stood by the door to the detective's office and Belkin sat in front of Morpello's desk.

"So who did it?" Morpello finally asked.

It was ten in the morning when Belkin got home. He was already starting to drift into sleep while lumbering through his apartment to the bed. By the time he got to it he was gone from the world of fires, Bibles, cops, winos, and murders. All those things lingered behind him somewhere as he shot into the second world of drifting images and oblivion. Commissioner Peyton had comprehended what Belkin had told them and started a process of inquiry. It was only a matter of time now. Detective Morpello was already getting credit for the whole thing before Belkin was even out the door of the police station. It didn't matter. On his way home Belkin had thought about the significance of fulfilling the Prometheus Vow. Always a life-changing accomplishment. Now he could get back to his normal life, above all to the Service.

He slept all through that day and night and woke up at eight in the morning to the phone ringing. It was Pernice Balfour.

"Detective Belkin! They have released me!"

"I'm glad to hear it, Pernice."

"They said you did it! I mean, that strange man, Morpello, he said that you were the one who figured out what actually happened! I can't believe it. I mean, you have been my only friend in this situation, Roy."

"Where are you, Pernice?"

"Well, I'm just outside the jail. They just let me out."

"Pernice, this has been a long road. A road full of scum basically. A kind of scum highway, or just a scumway."

"What?"

"I don't know. I'm just rambling. I've just about had it. I'm really glad you're out, though."

"I owe you everything, Roy. You and Lord of course."

"Of course."

"Roy?"

"Yes?"

"Would you like to pray?"

"Nothing would make me happier."

Roy heard some pages flapping in the background. Of course she must have had her Bible with her when they booked her and now that they had released her she was on the other end of the phone line with MY COMFORT. Her voice returned but with a very sonorous and hollow sound to it, as if she had one foot in another universe.

"Yea verily, my son, I sayeth unto thee, until thou doth returneth therefore ye to Absalom, all the flesh of thy forefather shall be like unto the very fruit of thy vengeance, for the blessed host hath been placed before ye, on this the night of thy remissions."

There was a silence. "Wow," Belkin said. "Is that from the Bible?"

"No, Roy, I just let the words come to me these days. I read a few lines and then just let His Spirit take over."

"Very strange."

"Thank you, Roy."

Before they got off the phone, Roy had invited her over to his apartment. He did it before realizing what he was doing. He gathered clothing and stuffed it into the closet and kicked small piles of papers and books under his bed. He picked up several dishes and simply stuffed them into the garbage. Really, the place wasn't in such bad shape, but this was the first and probably last houseguest he would ever have, so he wanted it to be perfect. Of course LeCroix had been over before but that was more of a home-invasion than a social event. He stopped cold for a moment or two wondering why he was able to pick things up without any of the usual power-building rituals. Pretty soon the house was all right. Then he sat at his window waiting. Finally there was a knock on the door.

"Roy, it's me, Pernice!" Roy heard from his seat at the table. Oddly, the sound of her voice was hard to place. It was neither inside the apartment nor outside of it. Also, it had a strange echo to it, as if she were shouting from inside a vast cavern.

"Where are you?" Roy asked, shocked by his own question.

"I'm out here, Roy! Right outside your door!" The voice had the same deep, echoing tone to it.

Roy got up and opened the door to his apartment. There was nobody there. He looked up and down the hall. Then he noticed that there was a large book on the ground. He recognized the letters embossed on the cover: MY COMFORT. It was Pernice's Bible.

"Pernice? Pernice?" He shouted. There was no answer. He took the book inside his apartment and set it down.

An hour passed. During the hour he got up several times to check the hallway again. It was impossible to understand. He looked at the book. There it was. It represented more nothing-ness than if Pernice had actually left nothing. The book instead of

Pernice was ultra-nothing. Where was she? Then he got out the Thunder Journal. He sat back down in his usual seat and looked at the last two entries he had made.

JAN. 14-
-THE DAY OF THE FIRE AND THE RELENTLESS POUNDING.
-ENCOUNTERED "SHE."

FEB 5-
-INCREDIBLE SLEW OF QUESTIONS CAME TO ME WHILE DOING THE SERVICE.

He wrote a new entry:

FEB 11-
-SOLVED THE CASE.
-PERNICE BALFOUR SAYS SHE'S COMING OVER, THEN LEAVES BIBLE OUTSIDE DOOR, DISAPPEARS.

He shut the journal and began thinking about what he was going to do with the rest of the day.

Belkin 345 asks: Did you know that in the Bible it says its okay to kill people?

Details: In the book of Aphos, 54:87 it says

"And God said unto Aphos, kill ye the first person that ye see, for that is the will of The Lord, even of The Lord of hosts. And Aphos said, Lord, why should I smite a man who have done me neither harm nor foul? And the Lord said, just ye do it Aphos. Do not asketh things of such natures as thus. Just ye do it."

Christ's_fool answers: What is the book of Aphos? Is that something you made up? You're crazy.

Theresamiller answers: Wow. Now that I know what "Aphos" thinks I am really going to go out and kill some people. Thanks a lot. LOL

LittleRob asks: What happens to people that die that believe in God but have not been baptized?

MountCarmel answers: God judges the heart after death. Anyone with a pure heart will be saved.

Belkin345 answers: If you have not been baptized they will laugh and laugh after you die. When you get up there they will all laugh and laugh. First they will open the door then they will slam it shut. Get baptized fast, even if it is just sink or toilet.

Belkin345 asks: I am spiritual man who tries bible every day and always keep thought very happy and pure. Yesterday I think I have accidentally raped myself. I am not sure but scared because there was a moist. What I do? What? Sin? Hell?

LittleJohn answers: Nobody respond to this. This guy is a troll. Pray for him but don't waste your time.

Disciple asks: I am trying to keep faith but having trouble. Out of money and also just had a bad break up. Keep trying to make things work but everything keeps getting worse. My hours just got cut at work and I have a disability that makes it hard to get a job. But it is a knee problem from my childhood so that I can't get disability payment for it. Keep praying and praying but things always seem to get worse for me. How can I get my faith back?

Belkin345 answers: Dear friend: Go with it. I mean, it's best to give up on the faith idea. Let me explain something. God doesn't exist. Tomorrow is going to be worse than today, as far as I can tell. I fell in love last month and the woman disappeared and left a bible at my doorstep. What is that? The only help I can offer you is that if you are interested in committing suicide but are too cowardly, contact me by email and maybe we can help each other up onto the ledge.

After sending the response Belkin sat there. It wasn't the first time this had happened. Lately, while doing the Service, he would find himself in a sudden funk and he would come crashing down from his usual euphoria and make a statement of real despair. It wasn't his style; it worried him. The Service was one of the few consolations of life. Now it seemed that his depression had crept into the very place where he traditionally found relief.

He shut off the computer. It had now been a month since he had resolved the Balfour case. Since then he had tried asking various people if they knew her whereabouts. He had tried the jail, his landlord, and people at the soup kitchen. Nobody knew anything. Father Basil hadn't seen her at all. All that remained was the Bible she had left outside his door: MY COMFORT.

Belkin had been modestly applauded after figuring out that Relpher was his own murderer. He had been in the newspapers briefly, though he avoided talking to any reporters. Beyond that, not too much had come of it. The police found the contraption that Relpher made to kill himself. It consisted of little more than a long, capped metal pipe—with a shell casing still jammed inside of it.

Knowing that Relpher started the fire in his own apartment, they were able to work backward and tie him to the previous arsons conclusively. And then, in a matter of days, the whole thing was virtually forgotten about as far as Roy was concerned.

He sat in his apartment thinking about everything. The Prometheus Vow had had little effect beyond solving the case. Whenever he had practiced it in the past he had seen some kind of change in his life afterward. This time he felt as though he had simply sat in a bathtub for twenty-four hours, attained one practical goal (solving the case), and gone back to being the man he had always been. This would have been more than enough if Pernice hadn't disappeared. Belkin didn't realize that he was so attached to sharing the outcome with her, to winning her over. Now that he knew, it was too late. It was this disappointment that churned in his thoughts and feelings as he lay down and let the afternoon and his own dark piece of it descend into a swampy sleep. He was awakened several hours later by a knock at the door. He roused himself and looked through the peephole.

It was LeCroix, wearing a green bathrobe. There was no shirt visible. His chest was hairless but inflamed—waxing. Belkin opened the door.

"Roy! You did it! You busted this thing wide open!"

"LeCroix, I can't talk right now. Please go away."

LeCroix walked into the apartment and sat down at the table. He was breathing heavily.

"Roy, the first time I saw you I knew you were different from other men—kind of a human rocket. But this, what you have done here, it's really impressive. I mean, I am impressed."

"Thank you, LeCroix. Do you know that I have a phone number? You could call the number. Just call it. Then I could answer it and tell you not to come over. How did you get into the building?"

Roy's voice sounded tired. LeCroix stopped panting and looked at him closely.

"Roy, you told me that your whole object in life was to clear your dirty little saint. Well, you've done it, Mommy. I'm proud of you. Babbith Marisol, who you met last week, is foaming at the mouth over this. I mean, Bud Morpello—probably the best detective this city has ever seen—he has said publicly that you deserve part of the credit for figuring this out. Everybody is happy, Roy. Why aren't you?"

Roy sat on the bed. "I don't know."

LeCroix stared at him quizzically. There was a pause. Then LeCroix spoke.

"Party."

"What?"

"We need to have a party, Roy!"

"No . . . no . . . "

LeCroix jumped up. The bathrobe threatened to flap open obscenely. "How could we forget? Let's see! I'll get Babbith, of course, and I think I can get some of my L.A. gang to come up. Oooh, Pomblo is back from Burbank! Watch out, Roy! You might just have fun!"

"No! No! LeCroix!"

It was too late. LeCroix slammed the door behind him. Roy jumped up and opened the door, only to see LeCroix receding down the corridor. LeCroix appeared to be skipping. Belkin was too tired to run after him.

17.

Another two weeks went by. The party didn't materialize though the threat hung in the air. The phone rang.

"Mr. Belkin, it's Steve Hoose, your father's principal handler."

"Yes?"

"He broke contact with us at six thirty this morning."

"Broke contact?"

"Yes. He has resigned."

"Resigned? What does that mean?"

"He has absented himself from governmental public service."

"What do you mean? Is he out on the lam? Did you let him out of the house?"

"He's dead."

Belkin didn't say anything. Steve Hoose went on.

"At six in the morning, Ulmers Belkin had a massive brain aneurysm. Attempt to resuscitate him proved futile. Agent Chalmers contacted our own special emergency—"

Belkin hung up the phone. He sat on his bed for a long time.

It seemed as though every feeling was taking place at once. The modern superstition of "the stages of grief" came to his mind. The first stage was denial. He wasn't in denial. He understood that his father was dead. Was he angry? He wasn't angry. It was hard to believe that his father was dead but not because of denial. He understood that it would be hard for him to believe that his father was dead for the rest of his life. Was he in shock?

He put the Shield on. It hadn't grown much. The only major recent additions were MANIAC NEIGHBOR and PISSING WINOS and those had been added a month ago. Since then he had left the house as little as possible.

The city was still out there. People strolled by. He noted that he had done no energy-building ritual but had just marched out of the house in a cavalier way. Was that shock? If so, could it be cultivated? He went to the intersection down the street where he always managed to be able to signal a cab. He decided he was in shock because he still couldn't feel anything.

At his father's house somebody buzzed him in and then there was a new agent outside the apartment door. The man had a face made of petrified wood. An absolute cigar store Indian with an earpiece. Belkin stood in front of him without saying anything. He was still trying to work out whether or not he was in shock. The agent didn't say anything. Like all the rest he had dark glasses on. Goings-on could be heard inside the apartment. Finally, Belkin spoke up.

"Ulmers Belkin was my father."

"Nobody is permitted past the perimeter."

"Can I talk to Agent Hoose?"

"I don't know who you're talking about."

At that moment Hoose emerged from the apartment. His hair was especially pressed down today, as if it had been coated with gelatin and then singe-dried.

"Roy Belkin, come in. This man is allowed past the perimeter, Agent Fife."

"Yes, sir."

The apartment was neat as usual. Calbenza was in a corner crying.

"Mr. Belkin, I suggest that you avoid the woman. She is level red right now. You'll want to come with me."

Belkin was grateful for the intercession. The last thing he wanted to do was to deal with Ms. Calbenza. He followed Hoose into the kitchen.

"Agent Hoose, I want to see his body."

"Roy . . . if I can call you that . . . " Hoose took off his dark glasses. The eyes were like ball bearings. "I know this is hard to understand. This is the exact intersection of protocol and tragedy. People get confused here. But this is something we definitely want to keep vapor-locked. There is no way I can give you permission to see him."

Belkin didn't say anything. He was still perplexed more than distraught. He didn't know what one was supposed to do, much less know what he actually felt. All he registered was a tingling sensation in his hands. Rage? Should he rage against Hoose? He didn't have the anger for it. Then Hoose spoke again.

"Mr. Belkin," Hoose said, and he placed his hand on Roy's shoulder. The gesture was very strange. Hoose was a man who rarely did anything human, much less intimate. "I am going to go talk to Agent Fife outside in the hallway. I am going to be out there for four and a half minutes. If I were to find you in that room when I returned it would be a disaster for our organization. Do you understand?"

Belkin nodded. Hoose looked at him again with iron implication and then slowly turned his back and walked out of the kitchen toward the front door of the apartment.

Belkin walked through the kitchen into his father's room quickly. Four and a half minutes wasn't much time.

His father's bedroom was the physical abode of a man who lived in his mind. The walls were completely lined with bookshelves. There were papers everywhere and many notebooks lying open on the floor. There were multiple hard drives, computers, and related devices piled on shelves and desks. His father's body was on the bed. He looked more or less the same as he had when he was alive. It was shocking and yet somehow consoling to see him. The thought of his father being dead was more upsetting than being exposed to the real thing. Belkin walked around the bed and started rooting through the drawers of the bedroom. He actually had no desire to see the body. Though he was in a bewildered state, an idea had come to him. There was something he had to find.

The room was cluttered but he felt that if he relied on his instinct he would be able to find what he was looking for. But it wasn't in any of the drawers. Belkin became more panicky. This was his only chance. A minute had gone by. He rushed to the closet. There were thousands of notebooks, documents, and old-fashioned brown file folders that expanded like bellows, each one overstuffed with the paper debris of calculation. He rifled through some of the stuff but what he wanted wouldn't be among papers. He looked under the bed. Then he checked in the drawers of his father's desk. These were mainly stuffed with cassette tapes and dog-eared paperback novels. Finally he sat down. About three minutes had gone by. Hoose was an exacting man. When he said he would be back in four and a half minutes that meant you could set an atomic clock to it. Belkin felt the pressure building. He couldn't think of anywhere else to look. As the moments grew short he had a last idea. He went over to his father's body. The body was clothed in pajamas. Funeral parlor language was rambling in his mind in a way that didn't make any sense. *Eternal repose . . . restful chimes . . . garden of joyous remembrance . . . chamber of memories . . . loved ones' consolations . . . graceful interment . . .* The lexicon of embalmment. A handful of marble roses. He unbuttoned the shirt on his father's body. And there it was. Of course, right where it should be! He didn't know why he had bothered to look anywhere else.

His father's Shield was a patched-together affair. He saw that it consisted of many layers of cloth, each one sewn onto the next until the whole thing resembled some kind of mad quilt. After all these years it was almost half an inch thick. The writing was tiny. There were hundreds and hundreds of listings. There would be time to pore over them later. Belkin ripped the Shield off his father's body, buttoned up the pajamas, and left the room.

He walked past Hoose in the living room.

"Good-bye," Belkin said.

Hoose nodded infinitesimally.

It was many hours later before Belkin took it out. It was something he didn't want to see during the day for some reason. He turned the lights out except for his desk lamp. He was at the very same table where he had spent thousands of hours at drinking cold coffee, worrying, planning, devising motivational strategies. It seemed appropriate to examine his father's legacy here. This table, more than his apartment as a whole, was his home. He took out the Shield and looked at some initial listings on it. They were written so small that many of them were completely illegible.

567. UNKNOWN AGENT OUTSIDE GARAGE

569. LOGARHYTHM 5-A FROM ABSTRACT ALGEBRA TEXT. DIFFICULT WITHOUT COFFEE. AVOID UNTIL IT IS FORGOTTEN ABOUT, THEN RETURN TO IT (WITH COFFEE)

570. THE EGYPTIAN LADY, STAIRWAY

571. AGENT KRESKY- NOT SO MUCH THE MAN BUT HIS MOODS

572. TELEPHONE, UNWANTED INFORMATION

Obviously his father was more broad-ranging than he was; he seemed to put any old thing on the Shield. As Belkin examined it he noticed the layers again. His father had added pieces when one was filled up, over and over. Roy carefully cut some of the tiny stitches in one of the outer layers and peeled back an edge. As far as he could tell there were at least ten more pieces underneath it. Each piece had forty or fifty listings on it. He skipped through them, unsure of what he was looking for. It was the first time he had experienced a sense of his father as a living person with a chronology. He began skimming down through the listings in reverse order, skipping many and just reading ones that caught his eye. He could do an exhaustive reading later.

431. AIR TURBULENCE—AVOID TALKING ON PLANE DURING—NAUSEA
427. STRANGE MAN IN AIRPORT (DANGEROUS?)
400. NUCLEAR THREATS/THREATS OF THREATS

When he would finish skimming a layer of the Shield, Belkin would carefully unstitch it to get to the layer beneath. It felt strange to be passing through the nineties and then the eighties year by year in such an odd backward navigation, all of it seen through a man's fears.

329. DISEASES SPREADING
328. FLY INFESTATION
327. MOTION SICKNESS
320. CEREAL—NIX WHOLE GRAINS NOW!

As Roy got deeper and deeper into the subterranean layers, the color of the cloth changed from white and beige to more weathered shades of gray and brown. The handwriting changed also. It was getting more meticulous as the entries on his father's Shield got older. Roy thought it indicated that what had started as an extremely careful process had become much more casual over the years.

216. AGENTS WHISKING ME INTO CAR TO AVOID—ASSASIN? BOMB?—FRIGHTENING WHISKING IN GENERAL
215. BUREAUCRATS SEEKING TO CUT OFF FUNDING
214. GAS
213. ANGRY CUSTOMS OFFICER
212. DYSENTERY (CUBA)

He could tell by the Cuba entry that he had dug through his father's Shield all the way back to the 1970s. He remembered Guantanamo Bay because although they didn't stay there long, it was one of the places where there were other families around. They had been at a military base of some kind.

160. 60 MINUTES TELEVISION SHOW—AVOID (PARANOIA)
159. BLUE MEDICATION HARMFUL WHEN INGESTED WITH PRESERVED FOOD
158. FRIGHTENING DREAM—SEA CREATURE
157. CURSING JANITOR (DANGEROUS?)
156. EGGS (NO!)

As he cut through to the very earliest pages of his father's Shield he realized that this was physically the very same Shield that his father had shown him so many years ago that day in the Philippines when he had approached Roy in the small cottage where they were staying, the day he had a bandage around his chest, the day he had warned Roy about the dangers of the outside world. Roy felt the heaviness of disconnection and loss that had taken place since then. He missed his father not because the man was dead but because he had been all but inaccessible while alive.

90. IMPOSSIBLE LEXIO MALIFICO CYPHER—ONLY USED BY ARGENTINIANS
89. GRAY EXTENSION CORD IN OFFICE OUTLET—SHOCK DANGER
88. JELLYFISH, TRIPS TO BEACH IN GENERAL

Finally, it was in front of him. Completely gray, barely readable, but he saw it: the first layer. Ulmers had never replaced it, just added sheet after sheet, year after year. The poignancy of the original time Roy had seen it returned to him. Suddenly Roy was in the Philippines, sitting on the floor looking up at his father. Ulmers was leaning over him, speaking to him as he had done thirty-five years earlier.

"You see, Roy, here's what you do. What you do, Roy, is you write things down that could cause trouble. If you write it down on this shield, it can't hurt you. See? That's how I do it. I write the things down on this shield and then they can't get to me."

8. MAN IN MARKET WITH SANDALS CARRYING KNIFE UNDER NEWSPAPER.

Roy lingered in the memory. It was the first time he had ever experienced complete sensory recall. He could see the banyan trees outside the window, and he saw that the walls of the cottage they lived in at that time were yellow, something he would never have been able to summon before this moment. Above all he saw his father looming over him, holding open his Hawaiian shirt and smiling, both paternal and terribly vulnerable. Roy thought about it for a moment more and then voluntarily departed from the vision. He knew if he tried to hold on to the recollection it would blur while he was looking at it, like an object one tries to scrutinize in a dream. Back in the real world he looked at the relic in front of him. The original layer of the Shield sat on his table with all the dog-eared strips he had carefully cut off sitting in a small pile next to it. Somewhere in the Philippines, with Roy the very small child in the house, the terrified man had created this totem to put something between himself and the world, even if it was only a talisman. Though Belkin himself had carried on the practice with at least equal superstition, he was able to see the strangeness of it.

Some of the early entries were unreadable but the very first one was clear. His eyes were drawn to it.

1. DRAFT IN THE HOUSE—BAD FOR ROY

Everything seemed to hold still when he read it, even the process of memory itself. He felt a kind of tremor in his stomach as his thoughts and powers of reason departed from him altogether. Flashes went off behind his eyes and everything solid broke apart into waves of warm black water.

Father Basil sat in the semidarkness of his office looking at Roy. Once again his hands were crossed in front of his face in a posture of absorption.

"When did he die?" Father Basil asked.

"Two days ago."

"And you want me to perform a Catholic service?"

"No."

"You are aware that I am a priest?"

"Yes."

"I understand. Your father wasn't Catholic."

"That's right."

"This is forbidden by my church. Is this going to be a gathering?"

"No. Nobody will be there except me and his live-in housekeeper."

"The only thing I can do is attend the gravesite and speak informally."

"That's all I want."

"You'll have to tell me a little bit more about you and your father so that I can know what to say."

"All right."

The room was dark and quiet. Faint noises from the kitchen could be heard below.

"And you still haven't found our friend Pernice?"

"No," Roy said.

They were in the emptiness again. Then Father Basil spoke.

"She was a very religious woman. Very sincere."

"I know."

"It could be that she was afraid of you distracting her from pursuing that life. The last time we spoke you said that she left her Bible outside of your door. For somebody as devout as her, that is a very meaningful gesture."

"Maybe. But she said *she* was coming over. She didn't say 'my Bible is coming over.'"

"Hmm. Well, you're right."

More nothing. Then the priest again.

"Tell me about why you did all this work, all this thinking for Pernice."

Belkin was surprised at having the focus put on him. He couldn't think of another time in recent memory when somebody had asked him about his personal motivations.

"Well, I guess I saw a kind of purity in her. So I made a vow out of it. You said that you understood that the first time I mentioned it to you. Don't you priests make vows? Vows of chastity and silence and so on? Well, I made a vow. I call it the Prometheus Vow. That's the most important vow in my world. Once I make the Prometheus Vow, it's a very definite thing. So then I kept working on the case until it was done. And now, I got her out of jail and she's gone."

It was more than Belkin usually said about his personal life to anybody. It was the silent air of Father Basil. You couldn't *not* reveal things.

"Why did you call it *the Prometheus Vow*?"

"I don't know."

"Do you know who Prometheus was?"

"No."

"He was the Greek titan who stole fire from the Gods, from Zeus, to give to the mortals."

"I just thought it sounded solemn. That's why I called it that."

"It may be that you chose the name for its archetypal significance."

"No, I don't think so."

"Maybe you have completed part of your vow but you haven't quite gotten hold of the fire, so to speak. Perhaps you have gone all the way to the doorstep, you have found it, but you haven't quite laid hold of it."

"No, I didn't even know about that story."

"The soul knows the old stories."

"Hmm."

"Anyway, perhaps your work isn't done."

"Okay."

The small office was floating in space with its books like a mobile star-library. The two men chatted in the vacuum.

"It could even be that you *have* laid hold of the fire, so to speak, but you haven't learned how to *hand it off* to the mortals."

"You're going too far."

"You're probably right. Even so . . . "

They floated.

The funeral, such as it was, took place in an annex of the military cemetery at the old Presidio naval base. There was a section for "civil soldiers" who by "performance of civic duties had greatly assisted the United States Military." This was announced in a plaque near the entrance that also stated that "there is more than one kind of hero." A couple of days earlier Agent Hoose had explained to Belkin that it was difficult to get a body into this lot and that the acceptance of his father was a big honor. The place looked fairly modest but it was probably better than what they did with unclaimed bodies—the landfill? Dissections? Belkin was relieved that he wouldn't have to deal with all the normal logistical problems of burial.

For one thing there was the manner of money. When Roy had talked to Hoose about funeral arrangements he had also been

informed that he wouldn't be receiving the monthly check he
was accustomed to. The conversation about the money had gone
like this:

"You won't be receiving any more checks after next month.
I'm sorry."

"Why not?"

"You weren't an employee. The checks were part of your
father's employment."

"Don't you military types take care of your own? Pensions?
That kind of thing?"

"We aren't military. Our network doesn't exist. I don't even
exist telling you this, which is the only reason that I feel comfortable mentioning it."

"Well, what about Ms. Calbenza?"

"She'll continue to work for us. We have other code savants
she could help with."

"It doesn't seem fair."

"I'm sorry. It's not personal. Protocol."

"It seems like protocol has been damaging me a lot lately."

"All of us."

The area of the cemetery where Roy's father was to be buried was
very plain. Trees were around. You could see the ocean if you
stood on a small mound near the back of the lot. Ms. Calbenza
was the only other person there besides Father Basil and Roy.
Hoose stood just off the lot and watched from afar. He had come
in a black town car. A driver sat inside, oblivious to the goings-on.

When Ms. Calbenza realized that Father Basil was a real priest she lapsed into groveling.

"Father, I are not worthy."

"Roy told me you were very close to his father, Ms. Calbenza."

"Yes, in the name of the Lord."

"God bless you, Ms. Calbenza."

"And you as well! And you as well!" Her tongue flopped around in her mouth. For a moment Belkin worried that she was going to go into the horrible gurgling and sputtering that he had seen her carry out in the one-room churches of his childhood, but instead she simply swayed back and forth like a reed. Then they got started. Some men showed up with the coffin (a pine box) in a truck. It was unloaded with a winch into the hole.

Father Basil spoke: "I did not know Ulmers Belkin but I feel that he is in the hands of that infinite Love that follows the ambiguities of this human life. We won't pretend he wasn't a troubled person. But he provided for Roy in his own way. Part of him is not lost. Roy persevered through all the phases of his father's illness, which started long before his physical loss took place. If there is a single measure of love, it is constancy in the face of problems and changes. As we say good-bye to Ulmers Belkin we do so knowing that Ulmers and the two people in attendance today formed a bond and a family that gave Ulmers comfort and a way to live."

Father Basil said a couple more things. Roy didn't hear the rest. He was mostly just relieved that there was some type of ritual rather than a purely physical interment, like the delivery of a heavy package into an open sack. At the end of it Ms. Calbenza left. She was crying. She walked out of the lot and got into the black car with Agent Hoose and the driver. Roy and Father Basil remained at the gravesite, watching her depart.

"There she goes. She's going to keep on working for those people."

"Roy Belkin, you are a good man. Don't be alone in the next few weeks. Come visit me soon," Father Basil said.

"Thanks for doing this."

"You're welcome," Father Basil said.

"Well, I'm going to go home. Maybe you'll get to do my funeral next," Roy said.

"Roy, did you think about what I said about your vow?"
"No."

Father Basil looked at him with his usual contemplative gaze. Roy waited for the priest to finish what he was leading up to, to say something like, "Well, think about it," but he didn't. Instead they walked out of the cemetery, said good-bye, and separated.

Roy went home. He sat in his apartment. His emptiness kept sucking everything into it so that even material objects looked like replicas.

The man was dead. They had never connected. It was a waste. Not the death, the life. Why bother? To solve codes? What was the point of that? Who was Agent Hoose anyway? What was *his* father like? Undoubtedly a prick, although Hoose himself wasn't so bad. What about LeCroix? What was his story? And what about he himself, Roy Belkin? The computer troll? He was the most deranged out of all of them.

Once on a television show Roy had seen, a therapist asked her patient to give a voice to his depression. The patient on the show closed his eyes and said, "Fire the therapist!" It was played for laughs because the actor said it in a funny voice. Belkin decided to try the technique, except only in his head. For a minute or two nothing came to him. Then he heard it: *Nothing has worked out, Belkin. Fuck you. Time for death. Come down here into the grave with me and your father. It's warm down here. All you have up there is more loss. A thousand more shopping trips. Bills are coming. The money is over. Come down here into the grave. I am your toilet. Jump into the big sad flush, crap-man.* Belkin stopped the exercise when he realized that it didn't have any therapeutic value.

He kept sitting there at his usual table spot. The sun was out. A bird was wheeling around outside the window. For some, this would be a time of cheer, just based on the weather. The paint was beginning to peel from the walls. In one hundred years it would all be chips. A new voice came into his head. It was similar to the voice of depression.

It is time to start planning the suicide.

The voice was frightening. Not because it was alien but because it sounded reasonable, like a voice telling him it was time to take a shower or turn on the lights. As if in response, he heard another voice.

"No, Roy!" It was Pernice Balfour.

"Pernice?" Pernice's voice reminded him of the last time he heard her speak outside his door when she had left the Bible. It was echoing, disembodied, and hollow.

"I'm over here, Roy!"

"Where?"

"Come to MY COMFORT!"

He looked around the room. He noticed the Bible sitting on

top of his television with the words MY COMFORT embossed on the cover.

"Yes, Roy! In here!"

Roy opened the Bible while looking around the room. It was definitely time for suicide. He couldn't take all-out madness. He absent-mindedly read the page he had flipped open to, still listening for Pernice's voice.

> *Oh, clap your hands, all you peoples! Shout to God with the voice of triumph!*

It was standard Bible foaming. But then after the initial bit of writing the text changed.

> . . . For the Lord most high is awesome; he is a great king over all the earth . . . *Yes, Roy, I am in here. After I got out of jail my soul wath tired of thith* Woeful plane and *it transmigrated into the only world that ever brought me joy, my Bible.*

Roy closed the book. He looked around the room. Death was coming—what difference did it make? He shouted into the air, "What are you doing in there? Come back! Pernice, I think I may have loved you!" The words came easily. After saying them he opened the book to a random page as he had seen Pernice do so many times. Once again, Pernice responded right from the written text on the page. The print spelled out not scripture but her speech.

Roy . . . don't . . . I can't leave the Book now. I am in here for good. It ith better thith way. I think I may have loved thou altho but my calling is not of your world. I have been called unto the light by the prophets of Absalom.

Roy slammed the book shut and said, "Well, can I still talk to you this way at least? Can I still talk to you in this Bible?" Then he opened it. She was still in the words.

Yes and no, Roy . . . my personality that thou callest "Pernice" is dissolving fast . . . so soon ye shall verily open thy Bible and not encounter me as Pernice . . . yet I shall always have unique words for thou . . . I shall verily be a light unto thy forehead but not as ye hath known me before . . .

He closed the book. "So that's it? You're going to live in the Bible? And I can speak to you, but you'll respond only in vague, disembodied Bible language?"

"Yeth," Pernice answered from the text. "I am turning into pure LORDWORD."

He put the book on the television. So it was real. She was really in there! But what good did that do him?

A week went by. Nothing much happened. He didn't try to communicate with Pernice again. He was terrified of trying to contact her and having nothing happen. Still, he was convinced that the initial encounter was real.

Everything was tedious. Each day he performed the Service mechanically and went through his old power-building rituals, but with diminished enthusiasm. People barely answered his stupid questions on the computer anymore. He had lost even the ability to annoy the religious types. There wasn't any life left in anything. Garbage was around. The Slow Evil was turning into simply the Evil.

The government checks would stop soon. There were bills, expenses. In a way, this was the real doom. Finance was the sword of every other bad thing.

19.

One day about two weeks after his father's funeral he talked to Pernice through MY COMFORT again. True to her word, she was still in there, but the personality known as Pernice had dissolved.

"Pernice! I'm still really depressed!" he shouted into the closed book, then flipped it open.

"Hencewith let all thine enemies be ashamed and confounded! They have no claim upon thy raiments."

"WHAT? WHAT DO YOU MEAN? IS THAT YOU, PERNICE?"

"Yeth! Make haste. Bear not the reproach of kings. All day thine own impertinence represses thou. Walk in my judgments. Fertilize the oak."

"PERNICE: IF YOU CAN HEAR ME, I DON'T KNOW WHAT YOU ARE TALKING ABOUT!"

"With thine own mouth make known thy blessed lament. Do not entrust riches unto the oxen. Build thee a jar of bread."

He tossed the book back onto the television where it stayed. Whatever had remained of Pernice was nowhere to be found. Her words were now as opaque as those of the real text.

He decided that he would end it. His idea was to put his head in the toilet and set it on fire.

That afternoon he threw Thuds into a wastebasket. He had to make five hundred in order to have the motive power to go out and purchase gasoline and bricks for the Self-Murder. The bricks would be to hold his head down—he was concerned that he might destroy the death tableau by removing his head during his throes. This couldn't be allowed to happen. He wanted his final act to send a definite message, not just leave an ambiguous mess. The world must find his charred skull in the bowl itself. His plan was to drain the bowl, fill it with gasoline, chain himself to the toilet, and stack the bricks on top of his back for ballast before striking a match. He intended to call the whole event "the Final Debacle." His plotting was interrupted by the phone ringing.

"Hello?"

There was no response on the other end. He heard only thick breathing.

"Hello?" he said again, and again there was no answer.

Roy didn't know what to do. He sat there listening to the breathing. Finally, there was a sound.

"Huh?" said the voice. It was Bud Morpello.

"Morpello?"

"Who is this?"

"It's Roy Belkin."

"Oh. I'm glad you called," Morpello said.

"I didn't."

"I've got a problem."

"I don't care."

"A man was killed. They killed him in a gym. They killed him with something."

"What's the problem?"

"He's dead."

"That's the problem?"

"I can't figure out who did it."

"Morpello, please, please just tell me what you want."

"Maybe you can cure it," Morpello said.

"Cure it?"

"Figure out the answer. Figure out who did it."

"You mean *solve* it?"

There was silence on the other end and then a sound as though the phone had been stuffed inside a hamburger. It was obvious that Morpello had one of his soft, beefy fists over the speaker. Then another voice came on the line.

"Roy Belkin?"

"Yes."

"This is Police Commissioner Louis Peyton. Wanted to thank

you again for your help on the Relpher case last month. Wonderful help. Thank you."

"You got it."

"Listen, I don't have much time. I'm working personally with Detective Bud Morpello on something and I want to make a proposal to you."

"All right."

"We have a homicide in the Mission District. We would like to employ you as an adjunct detective. It's very unconventional to do this but Detective Morpello seems to think very highly of you and what he says pretty much goes around here."

"All right," Belkin said.

"You'll do it? Just like that?"

"Well, I don't really have much else going on. I was planning to kill myself but there's no rush as far as that goes."

"I see, haha. Well, we can only offer you a modest stipend but if you manage to help us make progress on this we can probably extend it and add some bonuses for time and expenses."

"Fine."

"Great. Thanks, Mr. Belkin."

"You got it."

"Meet us at Sweat Time gym on Twenty-Third and Valencia at noon tomorrow."

"All right. One question."

"Shoot."

"Do you have Emile LeCroix shooting the crime scene photos?"

"Yes, as a matter of fact."

"Good. He's the best damn crime scene photographer in this city and I'm going to need him on the job."

They hung up.

He gave up his suicide plans for the moment. They could wait until he was done with this.

That afternoon Belkin decided to go talk to Father Basil. Since he had already landed several hundred Thuds in the wastebasket earlier, he had enough energy to just get dressed and go. He walked out the door and headed for the soup kitchen.

When he got there Father Basil was in a garage adjacent to the storefront. The garage was part of the soup kitchen's property. Father Basil was sorting through a giant box of clothing. He was taking items out of the large box, assessing them, and then tossing each garment into one of three smaller boxes. The oily-nosed woman whom Belkin had seen before was helping Father Basil.

"Roy! Fantastic!" Father Basil said.

"Hello."

They went upstairs. The priest seemed happy to see Roy for other than sentimental reasons.

"How are you feeling?"

"Bad."

Father Basil nodded. Roy spoke.

"I found Pernice."

"You did?"

"Yes. She's in the Bible."

"What?"

"She appears in the print on the page when I speak to her out loud."

"Hmm."

"Have you ever heard of anything like this happening?"

Father Basil paused for a moment and then took a pair of glasses from his desk drawer and walked over to one of the bookshelves in the office. His charcoal-black hands drifted across the backs of the books on the shelf as if he was reading Braille. After some browsing he removed a book and returned to the desk. As Father Basil flipped through it, Roy could see the title on the spine: *Stigmata and Other Physical Anomalies of the Devout*. After a few minutes the priest found what he was looking for. He walked around to where Roy was sitting and pointed out a passage.

In some cases, particularly in the Eastern Church, transfiguration of ascetics has taken on a linguistic dimension. Monks have been said to have inhabited sacred texts where they miraculously appear in stories, or speak directly from the printed word to other monks.

"There you go. That's it. That's what's happening," Roy said.

"Amazing!"

"I guess."

"You should write down what you see."

"I don't think so."

"Well, it's remarkable if what you are saying is true. Then again, you're grieving two losses. You're under pressure . . . "

"It's not a hallucination."

"I believe you, Roy."

"Thank you."

The priest walked back around his desk and sat down. Roy had the book in his lap. Father Basil leaned back in his chair. The chair creaked loudly.

"I'm working on another crime."

"Another crime happened? In your building?"

"No. The detectives called me."

"Oh."

"They have another case."

"Maybe it's a good thing to work on," Father Basil said.

"Do you think?"

"I don't know. Only you can say."

"Well, I'm going to the crime scene tomorrow. It will give me something to do."

A strange feeling came over Belkin as he said *it will give me something to do*, like the feeling one gets when one looks through the vapors rising from asphalt on a hot day. A thought emerged from the haze. He realized that he had a special talent. His power was that he was able to commune with dead souls, in a sense. That was why he had been so adept at reading the remaining objects connected with Frank Relpher, to understand the emotional life of the man from the things he left behind, where others just saw insignificant remnants. Just as the scraps left over from Frank Relpher's miserable life had told Belkin things, so this next murdered body would speak to him through the scraps surrounding the husk, he thought. A photo, a shoe, a room, maybe nothing. If there was nothing, it would be enough. The reason he could listen to the dead was because he was half-dead himself. Father Basil didn't say anything but his silence was that of listening rather than apathy.

"By the way, I think you're right," Roy said to Father Basil.

"About?"

"About the Prometheus Vow. I'm going to listen to the ideas

that come up from this next crime scene. That will be the extension of it. The fire, so to speak."

"Well, I think if you're doing something that brings you out into the world, then you must be on the right track. You seemed to have had very good instincts with this last matter of Frank Relpher."

"Maybe so."

"Do you think you are ready for something like this?"

"I think I'm not ready for anything else."

"Well, if it helps, I make most of my decisions by process of elimination," Father Basil said.

"I've eliminated everything."

"That can be an enviable position to be in."

"Maybe so," Belkin said.

20.

The next day Roy walked out of his apartment and down the hallway. The visit with Father Basil had given him what he was looking for: resolution. This was the fire he was going to bring to the mortals. Father Basil had been right about the vow.

This would be the continuing work, at least for now: to listen to the whispering bodies. A man had been killed in a gym. He would pick up inferences of how the man in the gym was killed and he would reconcile that man's death with the world of the living, help resolve the leftover trouble.

Roy and Pernice were never really meant for each other. He saw now that she was only a lure. The vow had its own ends. The fire of the gods was his ability to cure crimes by communing with murder-debris. There would be other bodies after this next one. That was the feeling he had. Who knew if the feeling was accurate, but it felt trustworthy for some reason. Anyway, at least for this next little project, his duty in life was to be an adjunct detective who specialized in corpse-whispering. As he walked toward the elevator he remembered something Father Basil had said more than a month ago, the first time Belkin went to see him: "If, when you wake up in the morning you want to be alive more than you want to be dead, then you have found something that works."

Belkin reflected in the long, dark corridor, moving toward the weak window light and the elevator. He noticed that he had forgotten to put on the Shield. He thought about how he had felt that morning when he woke up, when he arose from bed knowing he was about to go investigate something. He had a purpose that was related to something other than his own obsessions. Did he want to be alive more than he wanted to be dead at that moment? With this new work and everything? The fulfillment of the Prometheus Vow? Meaning? All that?

He said the answer out loud as he stepped into the elevator.

"Almost."

Then the steel doors closed and the elevator lurched downward toward the street.

Printed in the United States
by Baker & Taylor Publisher Services